# Sorrow's *Mate*

By Lowan Anderson

# DEDICATION

For my mother, Dee, who made me believe I can do whatever I put my mind to and my dad, Freddie, for teaching me that anything worth having requires hard work. To John for awakening new dreams. Finally, to my boys, Isaiah and Elias, for reminding me that our imaginations can create endless possibilities. You truly are my superheroes!

Published by Lowan Anderson

Editors: Angela Dodson & Clarence V. Reynolds
Cover Design/Graphic Designer: J Alex Blane

ISBN 13: 978-0-615-85131-0
ISBN-10: 0615851312

*except where permission was sought and granted

# CONTENTS

Lowan Anderson

# CHAPTER ONE

Darkness claimed the sky, crept along the sidewalk, and blanketed the homes that lined the street. The streetlights at each corner barely made a difference in the night. Her home was in the middle of the block, and by the time she reached it, she could barely see anything more than a few feet away. She could hear the loud laughter of some young men up ahead, and she smelled the smoke from their cigarettes as the breeze carried it up under her nose.

Finally reaching the house, she grabbed the railing and walked slowly up the steps. The large bag she carried bounced against her thigh with each switch of her hips, and something hard inside dug into her leg. Too tired to reposition it, she moved a little slower to ease the impact.

It was often late when she got home, but tonight seemed darker than any other did. She couldn't find a star bright enough in the sky or even a firefly close enough to shed light. She opened the first door to the corridor of the apartment building. Her apartment key was already in her hand, thankfully, but using it to unlock her door proved arduous. Gia finally crossed the threshold after pulling a double shift at the hospital.

She had spent sixteen hours caring for four patients, two of whom were incontinent, one who experienced the Sundowners' syndrome that sometimes comes with dementia each evening, and another who was too young to be occupying a bed on the oncology unit. Gia's whole body ached from the turning, lifting, and moving at a jogger's pace during the day.

An old man had said to her, "The best piece of advice I can give you, is never buy anything you don't have the money for. I lived during the time of the Great Depression, and because of it, my wife and I only had one child. Sometimes, now, I wish we had more, but it would have been crazy to have more than one. Hell, in those days one was almost too much. It was a hard time, and credit ruined a lot of people."

Gia listened intently as she did with every patient. She kept every story dear to her heart because these were the confessions of lifetimes coming to their finale. Sometimes, the talks were desperate efforts by patients to leave something of them behind in the world. She would give them that satisfaction, although her job was simply to keep them clean.

The little girl with cancer was extremely talkative and playful, not customary for this environment. She told Gia all about her friends at school. She had been playing at school when she fell down, causing a very severe gash on the back of her head that bled profusely. School officials called an ambulance to take her to the hospital. She had to have blood work done, and the results came back as "abnormal." Further testing revealed that she had a common type of leukemia that often occurred in childhood.

A small Asian girl, she never mentioned her illness to the caretaker who brought fresh towels and changed the linen. It was the girl's young mother, holding a baby no more than a year old, who had confided in Gia. Only once did the girl address her hospital stay, when the mother walked out of the room after tears began to well up in her eyes. "She thinks I'm going to die," the girl said. She never stopped drawing on the paper that was in front of her. She didn't even look up from what she was doing to see how her caretaker responded.

Gia didn't speak. She reached over and moved a strand of black hair that had fallen in front of the girl's face, and then moved on to the next room with the incontinent patients, passing on her way the girl's mother, who was still weeping .

One of the patients was so heavy that she required Gia to use every muscle she possessed to turn her. It took two of them, her, and a nurse , to do nearly everything required for this woman's care. All the while, Gia smiled and never wrinkled her nose at the pungent odor that came from the woman's cracks and crevices. Gia never wanted to make the patients feel more uncomfortable than they already were with cancer invading their bodies.

Tonight, she hardly had the strength to close the apartment door behind her, so she pushed it slowly, quietly, and not so deliberately. She was usually much faster about coming home and decompressing. Now, nothing seemed to motivate her. She walked slowly into the living room and laid her keys and purse down on the counter that separated it from her kitchen. She peered into the sink on the other side. The faucet dripped, and a puddle of water surrounded the two cups with iced tea residue and the one plate that would have to remain soiled until she could rest.

She had to stop her mind from bouncing around in her head like it was a pinball machine. She thought about the two-day old spaghetti in the refrigerator, and her rumbling stomach reminded her that the "sundowner" had become restless and combative at the exact time Gia had hoped to grab a small bite to eat. When she was finally able to calm him, it was time to collect her next set of vital signs, clean up the two incontinent patients, and turn them so that their bottoms would not chafe.

She missed her only opportunity for sustenance. She rarely had time for breaks, even on days when patients did not need as much attention. Now, she prayed for the strength to set the spaghetti on the stove, warm it up and hope to remain awake long enough to eat half of it.

"I can't," she said in a hoarse whisper to herself.

The spaghetti would have to wait. She turned and surveyed the living room, which was also the dining area. It was as orderly as such a forlorn abode could appear. The water-stained ceilings bowed and curtsied in corners that had been spackled over numerous times to conceal the damage, because the landlord could not or would not fix the roof.

Her second-story apartment was one of two in a row house like many in the Wilmington area that was owned by a slumlord. He had done just enough to satisfy the requirements of Section 8 without making any real investment to the property. She looked at the windows, frosted with something that would not come off. Not even with the fine-grade steel wool she purchased at the hardware store and used for hours.

The hazy film that remained distorted the view and made it impossible to distinguish what she was looking at on the other side at any given moment. It was probably a blessing and a curse, considering the view was of a small patch of earth with bits of grass here and there, speckled with everything from condom wrappers to needles left by the streetwalkers as they crouched low in the night. They used a large stone wall that rose up out of nowhere on the side of the house because it concealed them in the shadows from anyone who might interrupt their transaction. The wall itself was an enigma. It stood alone, serving no real purpose, and ran between her home and the one to the right of it, ending at the sidewalk. Perhaps someone built it to create privacy, and so it was being put to good use.

Drug addicts among the prostitutes used belts, socks or whatever they could find as tourniquets. They searched bruised arms and collapsed veins for a place to inject their poisons. If anyone walked outside, the person could smell the odor of cooked crack making its way up the wall and to the stairs that led to the front door of the apartment.

Gia hated that her young niece, Anita, witnessed the acts of prostitutes and drug addicts so frequently. The child had often pointed out the intruders, "Auntie, they're out there doing stuff in front of our house again." Sometimes, the women lay there half-dead, and several times she had called ambulances for someone she thought might actually be deceased. The women of the night blew kisses below the men's belts. Lips wrapped moist and warm around the member and vacuum tight smacking, with each kiss and growing faster and faster. Every now and then, the women would utter encouraging words of "come for me baby," or request of "deeper…deeper." He would spill his emotions into a condom or onto eagerly awaiting, pursed lips for the less cautious.

Other times, men stood as women bent over

in dresses or skirts that left nothing to the imagination. They usually moved fast and hard. Sometimes they inflicted more pain than pleasure, evident by the flinching and withdrawal of the receiving female. Some would announce, mostly for their own benefit, things like, "I'm tearing this up" or "This is some good shit." Some patrons took precious time with their purchase, pecking away at soft breasts that hung low under blouses without the benefit of brassieres. Hands traced curves and kissed breadnut-colored skin.

Sometimes, Gia wondered if the man was one of the prostitutes' ex-lovers reminiscing about a beautiful woman he once knew in her prime. With his eyes closed, he could still see the image of sparkling white teeth behind full lips that shined with cherry-flavored gloss. Once the two lovers finished, he would plainly see that her beauty had long faded after years of abuse by those who could not see her worth. He would pay her what he owed and leave the evidence of his indiscretion on the patch of dirt directly outside the window of the first-floor apartment.

Condoms, wrappers, assorted plastic bags all littered her front yard. Thanks to the frosted window, Gia could pretend the colorful array was a bed of flowers...

As she nodded off, Gia's head dipped down just long enough for her to jerk it back in the other direction. She had fallen asleep standing still. Making her way back to the bedroom, she put a hand out and used the wall for support. When she reached the door she heard a noise, then it was stifled. She closed her eyes hard and opened them again to wake herself, fearing that she may be dreaming, standing right there at her bedroom door. Again and again, she heard the noise, a little louder each time.

The bedroom door was closed tightly, and her mind struggled to keep up with what she was hearing. She heard a voice, a familiar baritone, proud and boisterous. This sound was one that she knew intimately. She grabbed the handle of the door and pushed hard instinctively.

She stared at the back of her man, Luther, dark, chiseled, and glistening with sweat. Gia watched him making love. He was an experienced lover, taking care not to dent or scratch. His back arched and the muscles of his buttocks flexed as he dived in, then he returned to the surface for air. He inhaled deep and exhaled with a grunt each time. He probably took extra care because his partner was a tender twelve-year-old. There stretched out on the bed, legs spread, eyes closed tight, and holding onto the chiseled arms of the baritone, was her niece. He rubbed his hands along the side of her small thighs.

"I love you baby," he said as he stroked her, "Oh, I love you so much."

"I love you, too," the girl whispered back.

Something inside of Gia cracked, and her chest heaved from the injury. This was the child she had taken in as a baby born too soon to a mother not yet ready.

Anita had been so small the aunt could hold her in one hand. As the baby remained on monitors night and day for three months, Gia had prayed over her bed.

"Walk with her, talk with her, and guide her.

Continue to bless her and keep her safe," was what she had asked God on behalf of the little girl.

Save the pale complexion, the baby looked much like the wayward sister who had given birth to her, as she lay there on the bed. Gia stood frozen, watching. Her mind was stuck and unable to move on to the next moment. She watched without blinking, without breathing, and without moving.

The legs of the petite girl gripped the muscular thighs, squeezing tight as he penetrated her. Gia watched as the tall man with salt-and-pepper hair buried his face in the child's neck and moaned in ecstasy. The girl wrapped her hands around his face, kissing him, the way a woman would. They caressed and loved each other with a familiarity that said it was not the first time. "How many times?" she wondered. How long has this been going on? Certainly, it couldn't have been long. Had she been so busy working that she missed such a betrayal happening right under her nose?

Their work done, they lay in each other's arms. It took just a moment for them to control their heavy breathing, and with the moaning now over, it was quiet enough to hear the cracking that continued inside of Gia. Then, each of them looked at her in horror as they realized she had been watching. Perhaps, at that moment, she was the aberration. After what she had witnessed, she should have been screaming as loud as the lovers next door who fought every night, yelling obscenities that most people reserved for the most serious offenses. She should have been throwing things with her arms and legs flailing. She acted neither as the scorned lover nor as protective mother figure in that moment. She was barely even human.

"Baby, it was just a mistake," he said, lying through his big pink lips. "She came on to me, and I tried to…"

The words faded into nothing as he realized she could not hear anything he was saying.

Standing there, feeling like an empty shell, she stared at the thieves who had taken any life left over after her grueling shift at the hospital. She stood still, as the niece, the pretty little belle, darted past her through the open door . The night gown that had been pushed up, now covered her body. He moved in closer to Gia, his hands outstretched and his mouth whispering apology and explanation. His eyes beckoned her to come nearer, to show some sign of weakness. She showed no feeling, no tears, nor anger, nor disgust. Perhaps if she had enough rest, she would have been able to summon emotion. Maybe she could have run after the niece, embraced her, and encouraged Anita to tell her aunt how Luther had violated her and forced her to participate. Had he also forced Anita to enjoy it and reciprocate with such tenderness?

If Gia had the strength, she would have pulled away from the touch of her man, the kisses on her face and arms. Instead, she stood like a zombie as the saltwater tears dripped from his eyes onto her face and entered her mouth at the cracks. His hands roamed the back of her neck and groped the small, round breasts, squeezing them tightly, trying to elicit some sign that she would forgive and maybe forget. Gia could not move, and for him that was sign enough.

He began the baritone melody again. He groaned as he massaged her body, as she stood petrified. He pulled the scrub pants down to her ankles from behind, and she could feel the lips play slowly down her back, lingering at the small space just above her bottom. She felt nothing until the face buried itself deep into the valley of her behind. At that moment, a single tear rolled down her face and fell to the floor. As if it was a signal to others, more tears poured down, and her chest began to quake.

She felt the tongue thrust itself deep into her anus as he squeezed her bottom with both hands. He played in the opening with his tongue, pausing to say , "I don't want anybody but you. You know I love you, right?"

He spoke to her softly and returned to suckling on her sweet spot . Finally, a sound escaped her lips. It wasn't the screaming accusations or curse words that should have come out. It was not speech at all. It was more like a song, a blues -- the deep, dark notes of a sad song that played between two people for so long it was effortless and perfect. Her chest quaked as the broken thing inside cracked a little more, but the song played on as he thrust the tongue over and over, and explored her with his hands.

He asked again. "You know I love you. Right, baby? Tell me you love me?"

As she grew warm between her legs, he withdrew his mouth and hands. He stood up behind her without speaking for what seemed an eternity. He grabbed her suddenly by both arms and forced her down onto the bed where the scent of her niece still lingered.

"You don't fucking love me? After everything we've been through, I make one mistake, and you act like I ain't shit!"

Gia could smell the alcohol that filtered through his pores. Her stomach turned as he forced himself into her and thrust violently. He pushed harder and harder without sympathy for the broken woman. He pushed until her body went limp and gave no resistance. He pushed on even after that. The odor of the aunt and the niece – and a mixture of blood and excrement -- blended together. Gia did not move an inch as she lay in the spot on the bed where the twelve-year-old girl had been only moments before.

Gia felt his manhood swell and convulse inside, as her empty stomach heaved. Saliva and yellow, bitter mucous spilled out of her mouth onto the bed. She did not move when he pulled out of her and kissed her forehead. She was still, as he turned and exited the room. She remained that way long after the front door to the apartment closed behind him.

On the other side of the door, Anita had been listening. She was both hurt and jealous as the uncle who had watched her grow into a young lady, and then taught her how to receive a man's affection, made love to her aunt, who had been a mother to her. Anita had run out of the room afraid of what was coming. She had almost been relieved to see her aunt standing at the bedroom door. Anita was ashamed of what she and Luther had been doing behind her aunt's back, while she was hard at work.

Uncle Luther had said," Your aunt works too much. A woman should stay home sometimes and take care of her man" as he took a swig from the bottle he kept tucked inside his back pocket. Flecks of spit flew from his mouth as he continued, "That's why a woman was made from man's rib, to stay by his side."

He expressed how much he needed her to take care of him in her aunt's place. Standing at the door now, Anita felt sorry for her aunt. She had kept the secret to keep Gia from being hurt.

Gia had been taking care of Luther and her. Her aunt's eyes wore dark circles and wrinkled slightly at the cracks, hinting at a hard thirty-nine years, but she had such a joyful personality that it was hard to tell her age. Aunt Gia was strong and beautiful. She never withheld her love and affection, no matter how hard the day or long the night.

Anita didn't want to steal the smile that Uncle Luther brought to Gia's lips when he placed his arms around her, or read to her aloud. She could see all of Aunt Gia's worries melt away when he rocked her in his arms to the sounds of John Coltrane playing "My Favorite Things." After all, the girl had felt the same way when she was the one being rocked to the penetrating music. The child never expected to hear lovemaking after her departure from the room.

Anita stood on the other side of the door feeling betrayed. She realized the hypocrisy in the sentiment, but it pained her even so. She heard her aunt sob and give in to the apologies and the lies. Gia didn't kill Luther, as Anita had often imagined her aunt would. More importantly, Aunt Gia didn't do anything. Anita could feel her stomach turn when she backed away from the open door, and her Uncle Luther walked out and left her aunt as she lay on the bed. He looked at Anita as he passed with a sardonic grin and continued down the hall toward the living room. He slammed the door shut behind him, and she looked back to the bedroom door. She heard nothing.

Anita walked into the living room and looked down at the orange-plaid sofa bed. She ran her fingers along the frayed corners and grew angrier. The tears that streamed down felt as if they would scald her face. Her whole body had turned into an inferno, and her heart raced. She covered her mouth with her hand to hold back the scream that grew into a golf ball in her throat. It seemed to block off her airway, and she could not breathe. She dropped down to her knees at the edge of the sofa and cried until the night grew colder and the tears on her face had dried to salt crystals.

Late in the night, her eyes were so swollen that she could hardly make out Luther moving as he re-entered the apartment and made his way back to the bedroom he shared with Gia. He noticed her sitting there and paused for a moment in the doorway looking down at her. She expected him to say something or do something. Before, he would never have passed by her without a word, or, at that time of night, a kiss and a clandestine touch. Now, he turned and disappeared behind the wall as though she were not there. He had looked right through her, an invisible girl, and he could no longer see her.

Anita stood and pulled out her bed. She reached under the sofa and removed the blanket and pillow. She tucked herself in and became lost in her thoughts. She had no mother and no father, and that day, she realized she was alone.

Anita  lay back in the bathtub with every part of her body from her shoulders down submerged. She turned over her pale hands and rubbed the pads of her fingertips, shifting the wrinkles like putty. The hot water she had run was now cold, and her hands felt much colder as she held one suspended in the air. Her body seemed foreign to her. She placed her hand under the blanket of water and touched her breasts, pressing until she felt the tenderness that had been lingering for weeks. She ran her right hand down her chest and onto her stomach tracing the midline to her belly button.

Letting her bottom slide underneath her, she let the water rise above her head slowly until she was looking through it. The loose coils of her hair fanned out around her face like seaweed in the water and swayed back and forth from the current she created. When her hair covered her eyes, she closed them tight feeling it graze her face and eyelids. She thought of opening her mouth and inhaling as fast and hard as she could. She wondered if she could keep herself there. Could she decide that the breath she had taken before going under had been her last?

The longer she stayed submerged, the more her eyes bulged out of her head and her chest felt as though it would implode from the pressure on her lungs. The force became so strong that it pushed her up and out of the water, and she gasped to fill them with fresh air. She caught her breath and slowly began washing her body. Rubbing the Dial soap over her skin, she followed by scrubbing with the thin, white washcloths that Gia brought home from the hospital. Anita rinsed herself quickly and then stepped out and wrapped herself with a white towel that was made of the same cheap fabric as the rag. She stood in front of the mirror, flossed, and brushed her teeth.

Noticing her chapped lips, she reached into the medicine cabinet for some Vaseline to smear on them. She closed the cabinet and was startled at the big brown pools staring back at her in the mirror. They seemed to go on forever and they were full to the brim with hopelessness and pain inflicted by anyone she ever loved, starting with the mother she never knew. She had seen the same look in photos of her mother and in her aunt's eyes, as well. Those eyes and the round nose were something the three of them had in common. The dark truth that lay within them saddened her. Tears began to form, and she hated herself for being so weak.

She heard a soft knock at the door. "Gonna be late," Gia said. Anita heard her footsteps disappear in the direction of the living room down the hall. She dried off quickly and splashed on some of Gia's White Diamonds perfume and her deodorant. Anita then fixed her hair, securing it in a ponytail that hung down her back. Her hair was very long with loose waves and curls. She thought she might be "mixed." She wasn't sure, because her mother never told anyone who Anita's father was before she ran off. Anita ran across the hall to the bedroom with the towel still wrapped around her and opened the dresser drawer where her things were. Choosing a set of sweats and underclothes, she dressed in just a few minutes and met her aunt in the living room.

"Are you ready?" her aunt asked. Anita shot a poisonous glance at her and rolled her eyes, moving toward the door without answering. Gia grabbed her purse and keys and followed behind her niece.

They walked out of the apartment and down to the bus stop on Market Street. It had no benches for them to sit on, only a sign and the storage building behind it. An older couple was standing arm in arm, as they did each morning on their way to work. They talked quietly to each other. The woman raised her eyebrows and spoke quickly, obviously chastising him about something. Standing next to them, a young pregnant girl was holding a toddler on the side of her protruding belly. The little boy looked around studying his surroundings, and when his eyes met Anita's, he smiled at her and bashfully turned his head toward his mother for protection. Anita wished she had grabbed a coat. The bright winter morning was frigid and the sweatshirt did nothing to keep her warm. She wanted to ask Gia how long it would be before the bus arrived, but she kept her lips closed, and the scowl remained on her face.

She put a lot of energy into making sure everyone knew how unhappy she was. The seventh-grade English teacher had sent her to a counselor who asked questions about how she was feeling and how things were at home. She kept her mouth closed then, too, because she didn't know where to begin. The day the counselor called home to speak with her parent or guardian, Gia had come looking for Anita after the call to talk. Anita never found out what her aunt wanted to discuss. Gia pushed open the bathroom door that day, but something about what she saw turned her away without a word.

Anita felt something against her shoulder, she turned to see Gia holding out a lightweight coat that she must have taken from the oversized bag she used as a purse. Too cold to refuse it, Anita grabbed the coat without speaking or looking her aunt in the eye. They never discussed the night Gia had walked in on she and Luther.

They arrived at Rodney Square and walked down toward the direction of Market Street Mall. Gia led the way, and her niece walked sluggishly and defiantly behind her. Anita peered into every shop window, interested or not, and took note of every item and every person she saw. She filled her head with meaningless thoughts to avoid thinking of her current situation. Her aunt turned the corner, and Anita followed several steps behind her as they walked one more block to their destination.

The tan, stone building blended with its surroundings. Nothing distinguished it from all of the office buildings and shops that lined the street. The glass door at the front was tinted so dark that it was impossible to see inside and the building had no windows. Above the door that Gia was holding open, was a sign with plain, light-blue letters that read: Planned Parenthood of Delaware.

"Hurry up, Anita. We can't be late," Gia said.

She had approached Anita one day. Gia explained that she knew her niece was pregnant and that they should "take care of it." Anita knew what that meant, though she never considered the particulars. She struggled with the idea that someone else had made the decision to "take care of" her baby. Not that she wanted to keep the baby, but because she was tired of others dictating what would happen to her.

Anita shifted in her chair as a lady in blue talked to her about what to expect, and at one point asked, "Do you still want to proceed?"

The question confused Anita. She wasn't there of her own accord. The choice had never been hers. Uncle Luther had taken that choice from her when she was seven years old. One summer day, as she waited with him for Gia to return from work, he bought her a Popsicle from the ice cream truck. He called her over to him and let her sit on his lap outside, watching people walk by.

He playfully tickled her under her arms and joked with her that her teeth would fall out from all of the sweets she ate. "You're gonna be snaggle-toothed baby girl!" he teased.

Next to them sat a beer and small bottle of dark liquor. When she finished the Popsicle, he brought her inside and talked to her about the way she had licked the icy treat and how she could do something for him that was just like that. He unzipped his pants and asked her to come closer. When she finished doing what he had asked, he told her to lie back on the couch. He got on top of her, rubbing himself back and forth until his body tensed. She could feel the thing that had been in her mouth rub against the orange and yellow panties. When he got up, she could see a small wet circle on the front of her undergarment.

Anita was afraid at first, then ashamed when her uncle told her she had to keep what they had done a secret. He told her that her aunt would be angry if she knew what the child had done. She didn't like keeping secrets from Gia. Luther bought her many Popsicles that summer, and he gave her other treats throughout the years. By the time she turned ten, the gifts had stopped, but she was no longer a virgin.

Anita could remember that orange Popsicle as if it was yesterday and she often wondered how things might have been different if she had asked for potato chips instead. Perhaps, she thought, her uncle would never have gotten the idea. Maybe she wouldn't be sitting here at the clinic, about to do what she had to do. Gia never asked her what happened. She had been content with the lies that painted her niece as a promiscuous and rebellious preteen. That was easier than facing the fact that Gia herself was in love with a monster.

At the clinic, Gia watched as her niece walked off behind the nurse. Just before they turned the corner, Anita looked back at her aunt.

"You're going down the same road as your mother," Gia had said to her. Anita's mother had walked away from her after seeing her face the first time. The day her niece was born, Gia's sister told the nurses she wanted to go out and smoke a cigarette. She did not come back. Someone called Gia down from the floor where she worked to the maternity ward because she was on file as the decision maker for her sister. The nurses explained what had happened. The whole day went by, and the baby lay in the NICU nursery. Through the glass, she saw the infant attached to wires, quivering involuntarily because of the withdrawal symptoms from the drugs her mother had been taking.

Now, as the nurse escorted Anita at Planned Parenthood, Gia could almost see the baby that she held close to her heart when she was finally able to take her home three months after her premature birth. She weighed just five pounds. Gia was afraid anything might bring harm to the hairy, brown-eyed baby. "Who loves you?" she would ask as she stroked the soft hair on the child's head and arms.

Gia had always been someone that her siblings could turn to after their parents died, but her sister and two brothers were young adults by then. She had never held a baby so tiny. Her niece would lay nestled against her, rooting in search of mother's milk. Gia would warm a bottle for her and pat her back firmly to burp her. Then Gia would hold the infant in her arms, rocking her and humming the tune her grandmother had when Gia was a child. That adorable baby would look up at her aunt with wide, brown eyes so innocent and sweet she thought God had sent down a tiny angel for her to watch over.

Those memories made her want to run to her niece and rock her in her arms, humming the way she did those first few years. The thought of her little niece on the bathroom floor, vomiting the day the counselor called, flashed in her mind. Gia had taken the counselor's concerns seriously and wanted to talk to Anita.

Too ashamed to talk about what happened the night she walked in on Luther and Anita together, she made Luther promise he would never touch her again. She had stopped working late at night, and when she wasn't home, Anita stayed with a neighbor named Juanita, who lived a few houses down. The love between aunt and niece was like a beautiful silk scarf. It was an accent that made two otherwise plain existences interesting and new. It was something others envied, to have someone to love you so hard. Gia loved her pretty niece. Perhaps it was because she looked so much like Gia's sister and felt so much like a daughter.

She never had any second thoughts about the role she played in Anita's life. She never regretted bringing the baby home from the hospital and signing documents to become her legal guardian. That was until she walked into the bathroom that morning and realized her young niece was pregnant. Gia might have thought about it sooner if she hadn't been so wrapped up in her own change of circumstances. She would have noticed that she had purchased too few sanitary pads and for three months had seen no accidently stained underwear that needed to soak.

After seven pregnancies over nineteen years, Gia had lost each baby in the second trimester. The first two had been too early to see anything that resembled a baby. But the others had actually been delivered with visible hands and legs. Two boys and one girl had been given a short funeral service which consisted of a few words spoken by hospital chaplains. With no money for a funeral and the little bodies so tiny, the remains were then left at the hospital for disposal. Two weeks before the counselor called to speak to her about Anita's emotional withdrawal and failing grades, Gia had taken a pregnancy test, and it was positive. As she was standing at the bathroom door, she realized that the baby that was growing inside of her and the one growing inside of the girl were fathered by the same man.

That morning at the clinic, Anita changed into the hospital gown and climbed up onto the exam table as instructed. The walls were painted off-white, and the room had institution-style green baseboards and trim around the door. A metal tray was at her side, along with a sealed package with a translucent blue film that contained instruments she had never seen before. Several long rods of increasing width were lined up together with three more instruments that resembled scissors with funny-looking tips. Another instrument resembled a duck's bill, but was much larger and made of metal. The sight of it caused a wave of fear to wash over her. She counted three metal bowls and red bags that she knew would hold items that would become bloodied by the ordeal. She looked around the room taking note of objects that were common for a doctor's office, such as the desk with the rolling stool, a blood-pressure cuff, and thermometer. She wondered how many girls lay here before her. She was warm and alive, but this place made things barren and cold.

A small, circular stain on the floor caught her attention. It was smaller than a dime and was just on the outside edge of the metal tray table. She followed the path of the light-brown spot up from the floor and back to the instruments. They had appeared inanimate to her before, but now the speculum wore an evil grin and even the upturned tips of the scissors sneered at her mockingly. She heard them taunting her, as she lay there feeble and alone. She thought of her own mother at that moment and wondered if she had sat in a room much like this one, hoping to rid herself of the parasite that was taking over her body. Maybe she had gotten up off the table and left, thinking she was saving the poor child. Perhaps if she had stayed there, Anita might have ended up being nothing more than a bloodstain to serve as a reminder that a foolish girl had gotten pregnant by a careless man. She hated her mother for not having the strength to end a life before it began.

Hearing a firm knock at the door pulled Anita back into the reality of the clinic room. The handle turned, and the door slowly opened. At that moment, she became resolute about the choice she was making for herself and for her ill-fated fetus.

# Sorrow's Mate

## CHAPTER TWO

The sun shone through the large skylight of the slanted loft ceiling. Two smaller windows were on each side, allowing more light to stream into the room. The colorful Native American tapestries that hung on the wall behind the bed made the room appear vibrant and rich. The light painted a trail across the room. The bed sat in the very center. It was a large loft with an open design. The kitchen was at the right of the entrance, and there was an island where three women were eating breakfast and quietly talking among themselves. They did not want to disturb their host.

The "bedroom" consisted of a bed, a distressed aqua-colored dresser, a small table and oversized Victorian armchairs, reupholstered with a regal-looking purple fabric sprinkled with gold specks. The white table between the chairs was decorated with a large turquoise-colored vase, a few novels, cookbooks, and books about religion and sex. In the vase were five daisies in yellow, purple, and white.

Just beyond the sitting area was the formal living room, with a brownish-red, leather sectional for company to sit on and watch movies or hold stimulating conversations, or even to throw a bachelorette party. Leftover ribbon and decorations from the night before still hung from lamps, while balloons in light pink, hot pink and purple were afloat at the ceiling. Empty wine and cocktail glasses were on the mahogany coffee table. The walls were a blue-gray, decorated with large canvas prints of photos the owner had taken herself and hung randomly throughout the space. One picture depicted a little orphan girl she had met in a Mexican village during one of her trips. Another showed a beaming, former drug addict she had heard singing as she walked through downtown on her way back from watching SuiteFranchon put on one of her poetry events at The Café. SuiteFranchon recited poems that spoke of true life, its obstacles, and prevailing over them.

The female spoken-word artist reminded Eve

of the militants depicted in photos of the Black Panther movement with her big natural hair and black attire. Her message had been one of cohesiveness among women.

Several songstresses whose voices and styles rivaled those of Jill Scott and Erika Badu were there too, along with several male singers whose soulful voices caused women in the audience to swoon and their eyes to narrow catlike, as if the song was just for them. Eve loved attending those performances in her hometown and supporting some of the people she knew, and others that she didn't.

The ex-addict was standing one block from the venue in front of the art school, and the soulful voice that carried its way up several blocks away from The Cafe moved Eve more than any of the performers inside of the building had that night. So she took out her camera, which she always carried with her, and snapped several shots of him. Throughout the loft were also several prints of landscapes of places around the world where she had traveled while working.

Eve rolled over, and one leg swung outside of the comforter and off the edge of the oval bed. She stretched and yawned at the same time, opening her eyes and squinting from the bright daylight that poured into them. The summer morning was already becoming uncomfortably warm, and the digital clock on the table read 7:32 a.m. Despite the heat, she could not sleep without cover. She tilted her head back against her pillow and let the warmth hug her face. She loved the light, and it reciprocated her love. Her brown skin never burned even when she spent hours outside, on days much like this one, in search of the perfect image. Instead, her skin resembled baked bread and glistened as if she had polished it with butter. A thought occurred to her, and a huge grin crossed her full lips. Her bright, brown eyes sparkled in the sunlight, and she said aloud, "I'm getting married today."

Her two cousins April and Allison, who were her bridesmaids, were already up and sitting at the cherry wood island in the kitchen on two of four bar stools that surrounded it. Her cousin Allison was leaning on the white countertop fidgeting with the floral bouquet that Eve would carry down the aisle. April and Allison were her first cousins on her father's side of the family. They were twins who grew up with their father and lived around the corner from the apartment where she lived with Gia most of her life.

"Good morning, girl, it's your big day!" said Jade, her best childhood friend and maid of honor, extending a tray to Eve as she sat up in the bed.

On the tray were several plates overflowing with strawberry-covered waffles, scrambled eggs, bacon, home fries with onions and green peppers, and orange juice. Her stomach began to flutter, and she started salivating the moment the smell of the food tickled her nose.

"I can hardly eat I'm so excited," Eve said as she picked up a piece of bacon from the tray and ate a mouthful of eggs. She then stood and placed the tray down on the floor beside the bed.

"I'm getting married," she squealed gleefully with her mouth still full.

The two cousins and friend joined in, and all of them danced a happy dance of their own in a joyous circle, sending up a chorus of laughter, until they collapsed like children playing London Bridge.

"We've got so much to do. We have to get started," April said as she walked to the wardrobe where Eve had carefully stored her dress and shoes several weeks before the wedding. April took the dress, covered in plastic, out of the cabinet and laid it on the bed. Eve had purchased the pearl-colored gown from a consignment shop long before she became engaged. It was the shop of a small foreign lady who had imported the dress from India. The bottom fell in uneven layers, and each layer was made of a different material -- lace, cotton and a sheer fabric. The top of the dress was strapless, adorned with rhinestones, pearls, lace, and stitched flowers in assorted pastel colors. A long, sheer train had been added. The dress was breathtaking. At the waist was a slate-blue sash with a pearl broach at the center. The shoes were modest lace high heels dyed to match the sash.

The bridesmaids each would wear a dress in the same hue as the bride's sash and shoes and in a style of their choosing to suit their different body types. The women began to prepare for the occasion, and professionals began to arrive to style their hair, apply makeup, and polish nails.

As Eve sat in a chair with her eyes closed while the makeup artist worked, she heard a light knock on the loft door. One of the bridesmaids went to answer it, and soon after she heard her mother's soothing voice in a series of oohs and aahs, expressing approval of the gowns and makeovers. Eve could hear her mother make her way slowly toward the Victorian chair where she sat, but her mother didn't say a word.

"Mom?" Eve called out, wondering what had caught her mother's attention.

"Yes, I'm right here," Gia spoke almost in a whisper trying to steady her voice as the tears formed pools in her eyes. She marveled at her daughter's beauty, grateful that it was more than skin-deep. Despite the shortcomings of the people who had been there to nurture her, Eve turned into a loving, compassionate, and determined being. When she saw something that wasn't right, she did whatever she needed to create change. Gia admired and envied her daughter's strength. She wished that she had lived her life that way and that so many things would have turned out differently. Tears of joy poured onto her cheeks. Eve opened her eyes and saw her mother crying.

"Oh no, don't start, Mom. You're gonna make me cry, too. I can't mess up my makeup already." Eve laughed and even her doe eyes seemed to turn up in a smile. The two shared those lovely brown eyes.

The stylist had swept the daughter's hair over to one side, where it tumbled down in dark-brown ringlets. She had brown lips, and the makeup artist was preparing to color them with a rosy-brown stain and gloss. The rest of her makeup was very light and natural. She needed little embellishment. The mother reached over to the white table, picked up a pearl necklace, and fastened it onto her baby girl's neck.

"Something new," she said. She then pulled from her purse a pair of charming aquamarine earrings, adorned with pearls. They were birthstones given to Gia many years ago as a birthday present. "Something old, something borrowed, and something blue." She placed each earring on Eve's petite ears, then stepped back to look at her greatest accomplishment.

With everyone dressed, they packed up all of the items they would carry with them down to the car.

At the door, Gia turned back, saying, "Oh, ladies, I forgot my purse. Just a minute."

She walked over to the white table and pulled a large, gold envelope from her bag and rested it against the vase. Next to it was a photo of Eve and Nathan standing in front of a waterfall. Her daughter was smiling her big bright smile, and he had both arms wrapped around her in a warm embrace. Gia turned and quickly walked out of the door, closing it behind her and joining the others.

The bridal party of five stepped into the cream-colored Rolls Royce limousine. A friend of Eve's was there taking photos as they dressed and entered the limousine. She would take more pictures of the wedding party after the ceremony. It was a sunny day, and the ladies glistened like bronze figurines in the sunlight. Each one excited and relieved that the couple was finally getting married. They had been prolonging the inevitable, quoting the age-old cliché "Marriage is only a piece of paper."

The truth was that each wanted to be with the other as husband and wife. As two children who had witnessed so much devastation, they were afraid of what the institution of marriage would bring to their extraordinary friendship. Eve thought back on the relationship between her and Nathan, which had spanned sixteen years, beginning when she was only twelve. When they met, love and marriage was far from her mind. She had been in a dark place, and survival was what she hoped for instead. He had come into her life at the worse time and pulled her out of an abyss that threatened to swallow her whole.

A smile crossed her lips at the thought. She felt like Snow White, asleep until her prince came along to plant the kiss that would awaken her. Their story had been much less like a fairy tale and more like one of Aesop's fables. Tragedy had been the signature theme, and with each unfortunate event had come a lesson worth learning. She was lucky to have come out of it all unscathed. Some had been less fortunate.

The day Nathan found her, she had been out on the streets for three days. She might have been considered a runaway, but she wasn't sure that anyone wanted or needed her back at home. The circumstances surrounding her departure left her in shock, and after three days without sleep or food, she was delirious. She walked away from the Brandywine Park, where she had slept in the woods and crossed over the bridge on Market Street that spanned the Brandywine River. She walked aimlessly and ended up standing in front of a liquor store on Vandever Avenue in Wilmington.

A fat, fair-skinned man with freckles pulled up to her in a car and asked, "Hey, honey, you need something?" She looked the man over, unable to respond to his question. She needed many things, but what she wanted at that moment was to go home to her mother. She wanted to ask Gia for forgiveness and beg to come home, but she thought that was never going to happen. So, when the man pushed open the door of the silver Hyundai Elantra, she got in and said, "I need something to eat."

The man smiled at her, baring his golden, decayed teeth, and he made a right turn onto the street at the corner. He didn't say another word until they pulled up to the KFC drive-through and then asked her, "What do you want?" She replied, "Can I have a chicken-strip meal and iced tea, please?" He repeated her order to the drive-through attendant. Once he paid for and received the food, he drove off and turned onto Interstate 495, heading south. He handed Eve the bag, and she bit into the chicken like a ravenous dog. As she focused on the meal in front of her, she didn't pay attention to where he was taking her. If she had to call someone to tell them where she was, she would have no clue.

After a while, he pulled up in front of a neglected row house; and on both sides of the street, women, men, and raggedy children lingered around idly. He said to her, "Come on here." She could have refused, but where was she going to go? He had bought her food after all, maybe he would ask her for her phone number and call to notify her mother that he had found her wandering around outside. Eve stepped outside the car and followed behind him as he walked toward the door of the row house. She looked up and examined the scabs on the balding spot at the back of the man's head. Dusty, red hair that resembled dirty cotton balls wrapped around the sides and back of his head, and the same red freckles covered his neck. The T-shirt he wore was grimy around the collar, and the same brown dirt stained the crease of his neck.

She noticed several young men playing cards at a table just outside the front door as she stepped inside. The house smelled of rotting garbage, cigarette smoke, and crack cocaine. She had smelled the crack when junkies cooked up around her apartment building. The familiar odor stopped her in her tracks, and she turned toward the door realizing that she probably should not be there. She felt a tight grip on her arm. She turned back to see that the man who had seemed pleasant now appeared much more like the boogeyman, and he pulled her down the hall in the direction of a dark room.

"No, let me go, I want to go home," she screamed, grabbing onto the doorjamb of the room. He squeezed her arm tighter until she winced in pain. He pulled her so hard it elevated her from the floor for several seconds, and then he dragged her into the room. Two other men stood around the room and both stared on with intrigue as the red-haired one threw the girl onto the filthy mattress. "Look what I found," he said,

She rolled over onto her knees and tried to push herself up, but someone grabbed her by her ankles and pulled her so that she fell flat on her stomach on the mattress. She looked to the side of her, and a skinny man kneeled at her side chuckling. His mouth was wide open. Crusty white patches encircled his lips. His breath was stale and hot against her face. A few of his bottom molars were all that remained of his teeth. He grabbed her head and forced her face down so that she was no longer looking at him. She could feel hands pulling at the denim jeans she wore. Her pleas to "stop, please don't" were swallowed up by the mattress stuffing, and she gasped for air. She felt fat, calloused fingers touching her between her legs and felt what she knew was a penis rub up against her privates.

Outside, a boy was sitting at a table in front of the house where his cousins were hanging out, smoking weed and playing cards. He had come to drop off one of the cousins after a basketball game. They persuaded him to stay and play a game of Spades. The afternoon was bright and cool, and the neighborhood was alive with activity but peaceful, unlike some days. Perhaps it was because of the cool, fall temperature. He had seen

the man they called Redman walk into the house
with the young girl. He didn't recognize her, but
that wasn't what caught his attention. He had seen
many girls follow the crack heads into the house.
Most of them walked with certainty, and were
there for a very specific reason, with no concern
about what was happening around them. This girl,
however, had walked slowly and cautiously behind
the man. Her eyes searched the surroundings, and
he could see the uneasiness in the way she
swallowed hard with each breath. Her eyes were
beautiful and innocent, big, brown eyes that told
the truth about her age, and the purity inside them
was in contrast to the place where she was
heading. Her eyes told him that she was, in fact, in
the wrong place and sensed that nothing good
would come to her there.

He did not act right away. Time and
experience had taught him that minding his own
business would help him survive. His
grandmother, Emma, however, had taught him
something else. She had been shelter and a safe
haven to many. Battered women, children,

homeless drunks, and even castaway crack heads had found solace with Miss Emma. She had taught him that life could turn bad for anyone, no matter how good it may seem at the moment. She reminded him always to speak to every stranger on the street. "You never know where you might meet them again," she said.

He was thinking of her when he placed the cards on the table and walked to the front door of the house. He had ignored the protests behind him. "Hey, man, how you gonna walk away now. Come on, man." Skepticism followed him all the way through the front door, but the moment he heard her screams he grabbed the baseball bat that was leaning against the front door. It was left there by the drug dealers who kept it for safety against fiends and envious competitors. He followed the sound of her voice to the bedroom. The sound the bat made as it cracked against their skulls and bones would have made him vomit any other time, but now the idea of it gave him comfort.

Suddenly, Eve's legs hung free, and she could

hear commotion in the background. She jumped up and watched as one of the young men from outside beat the three old men with a baseball bat. He screamed out as he beat them, "Nasty... Fucking rapist...Dirty bastards!" By the time he had finished his work, the men lay bloodied and sprawled out around the room.

With each blow he had grown stronger, and the more the men screamed, the more he wanted to hear their cries. The poor girl lay there on the bed as these beasts forced themselves on her. He knew that one of them had several granddaughters that looked to be very close to her age, and it sickened him to think the man could do such a thing. He never stopped swinging the bat until the last one stopped moving or making a sound.

Then, he remembered the captive, who had slunk away into the corner. When he looked at her, he could see fear in her eyes, and he realized she was afraid of him now. Rightfully so, if he hadn't been looking for her, he might have swung his bat until everything in the room stopped moving. The moment his eyes met hers, he remembered himself, remembered his grandmother Emma, and remembered he had come into the house to bring her out.

He couldn't take his eyes off of the girl, who had retreated to the corner and curled up into the fetal position. Eve was afraid for a moment because he had the same wild look in his eyes that Redman had when he grabbed her arm in the hallway. Almost as though someone flipped a switch, her defender's eyes went soft, and she thought she saw tears in them. When he walked over to her and extended his hand, she took it, and he pulled her up. "Fix your clothes, and then come outside. I'll take you home."

He walked out before she could respond, and she did as she was told. She moved slowly through the house, afraid that another boogeyman was hiding around any corner. When she stepped through the front door, the young man was waiting for her as he promised. He wiped away a spot of blood from the corner of her mouth, and she felt a sting where the skin had torn when the men smashed her face against the mattress. Then, he placed his hand on her shoulder and gently prodded her in the direction of a white Nissan Altima that was parked several homes down. She sat in the passenger seat and put on her seatbelt.

"Where do you live?" he asked her politely.

She began to cry for the first time since before she left home. "Nowhere. I don't live anywhere."

She didn't make eye contact, but she felt his dark eyes piercing through her, and it made her cry even harder. He raised her chin with one hand and wiped away her tears with the other. He pulled out of the parking place and drove off. She still had no idea where she was but saw a sign for the development that read Brookmont Farms as they were leaving. She had heard of the area before. It was similar where she lived in the city, with a large population of Section 8 voucher recipients mixed in with blue-collar homeowners.

They drove for about ten minutes in the car, before he asked, "What do you mean you don't live anywhere?"

He had given her time to calm down. He was sure she had been through much more than what he had witnessed. Only someone desperate and without options would have followed Redman into that house.

"I can't go home. I did something terrible, and I ran away," she answered.

She didn't look him in the eyes. Shame weaved its way through her words, but it wasn't shame for what he would have thought. He'd seen her laying there with her privates exposed as filthy junkies touched her with their hands and genitals. Dirt, remnants of food and greasy finger marks caked the walls of the room. Cockroaches roamed freely throughout the room, including on the bed and mattress where they held her down. Yet there was something much more vile and degrading about her that she was ashamed for him to know.

She simply said, "I can't go back there," as the car pulled up in front of a small ranch-style house with a nicely manicured lawn.

She got out of the car and followed behind

him without any invitation because she felt safer with him than she would have alone. He unlocked the front door, and she walked in behind him. The house was clean with minimal and modest furniture, but she felt at ease there.

He said to her, "Wait right here for a minute."

Then he disappeared through a doorway to the kitchen. He returned with a small, elderly woman who wore thick glasses and a friendly smile. In her hands, she carried a pair of pants, shirt, socks, towel, and washcloth.

"Here, Shuga. Follow me and I'll show you where the bathroom is. Lord knows you could use a good scrub down."

The lady led her into the bathroom and turned the faucet to begin running a hot bath. She turned back to the girl and studied the young face. "I'm Emma, and my grandson Nathan tells me you don't have no place to go." She paused looking hard at the brown-eyed girl over the lenses of her glasses. "You can stay here, but I'll need to know who your folks are, so I can let them know you safe, even if they don't care to know."

Eve showered and got dressed in the bathroom, putting on the clothes that Emma had brought for her. When she came out, she could smell the aroma of something baking and something frying. When she walked into the kitchen, she saw the woman standing over a large pot on the stove, stirring greens with smoked turkey parts throughout. Eve grew hungry again immediately.

"Sit down, darling. I'm about to fix you a plate in just a minute." Eve looked outside the window and noticed the car was gone.

"Where did he go?" she asked.

"Oh, he'll be back, I sent him to the store to get me some tea bags," Emma said. The small woman's arms moved about the stove like a maestro conducting a wonderful orchestra, and when she was done, she brought over a large plate of food and placed it down in front of Eve. Miss Emma had piled the plate high with a piece of a roast smothered with gravy, next to potatoes that were cut up and seasoned to perfection with onions, tomatoes, and garlic. Eve tasted the greens first because she wanted them the moment she saw them in the pot.

Miss Emma came back to the table carrying a plate with a buttered biscuit, and she sat down in front of the girl staring intently at her eyes. "Take your time and eat, that food ain't going nowhere."

After Eve finished her meal, Emma cut her a slice of 7Up cake, and although the girl had no room left in her stomach, she forced down every bite for fear she would miss out on a delicacy if she didn't. When Eve finished eating, Emma guided her guest into the living room, and they sat on the floral-patterned sofa.

Emma turned to Eve and said, "Now, we've got a lot to talk about. Take your time and start from the beginning, sweetheart. What's your name?"

"Eve," she replied sheepishly.

Despite Miss Emma's small frame, something about her seemed large and intimidating. Still, when she reached out and placed her hands on the girl's face, Eve relaxed and the story spilled from her lips. When Nathan returned, the girl was in tears and hugging his grandmother for dear life. He went into the kitchen and sat the bag down on the counter. He took out his purchases, placing yellow roses that Emma loved so much in a vase and filling it with water. Then he took out a small bunch of mixed-colored daisies and handed them to the girl.

On her wedding day, Eve now smiled at the memory of sweet Miss Emma, who had passed away more than ten years ago. At that moment, the limousine pulled up to the Fifth and Central Presbyterian Church. She stared up at the majestically constructed brick building with large white columns on both sides of the doors. A tall, white steeple housed a bell at the very top. Inside waiting, stood the man she was about to marry. They had met at one of the worst times of her life, and Nathan had turned out to be one of the best things that ever happened to her.

The driver approached the door and opened it, stepping aside to allow the women to pass. The two cousins got out first, April holding Eve's bouquet, followed by Jade, Gia, and lastly Eve. The bridesmaids helped her step out carefully so as not to soil the drop-dead gorgeous gown. Allison, who had been holding the veil, clipped the jeweled piece onto Eve's hair at the top where it flipped to one side and pulled the veil down over her face. They climbed the stairs to the entrance of the church. Eve turned to Gia, who had begun crying again. She lifted the veil and put both hands on her daughter's face. She was so happy that she was able to participate in the wedding. She had been afraid she might be unable to be there to support her child and to enjoy the good time that had finally come.

Gia's wrinkled hands resembled her own grandmother's. Eve ran her hands along her mother's silver dreadlocks that had been styled into a bun at the back of her head. Gia had aged well, but now, as she approached almost seventy years old, time was beginning to catch up with her. She was almost forty when Eve was born. Gia's skin was a milk-chocolate brown and had lost its moisture over the years. Still, Eve could see parts of herself in the attractively aged woman who was staying active and keeping her figure intact. She looked regal in the gold, fitted dress with the multicolored scarf that draped around her neck and over her shoulder, matching the colors of the bride and the wedding party.

Eve wiped the tears from her mother's eyes and leaned in to peck her on the cheek. "I love you so much," she said.

The tears came harder. "And who loves you?" Gia asked her daughter the question she had asked her as a baby until she had gotten too big to be amused by it.

This time, Eve said proudly, "You do."

Gia then replaced the veil over the bride's eyes and the doors opened so the mother and then each bridesmaid could glide down the aisle. When the musician began to play "Here Comes the Bride" Eve stepped inside the sanctuary, and she could hear the 250 guests gasping and singing her praises. She looked ahead and at the altar, waiting for her, with the biggest, brightest smile, was her Nathan. He looked at her and beamed with pride.

The woman walking toward him was the most wonderful person he had ever met. She was intelligent, kind, and resilient beyond measure. All of his hopes and dreams were merely tools to procure the means to keep her happy. She was his happiness and all he would ever need.

# CHAPTER THREE

Two little girls stood opposite each other turning a rope in each hand, while a third child stood to the side, rocking back and forth and waiting for the perfect time to jump between the spinning ropes. On the ground nearby was a pattern of squares drawn with chalk where they had played hopscotch earlier in the day.

Eve spent the entire summer with her cousins April and Allison, and her friend Jade. They bickered over toys and over who was faster, taller, or better at something. Mostly, they laughed, played double Dutch or hopscotch, and skated up and down the block. Sometimes they played kickball in the parking lot of the storage building across the street.

"I'm gonna be five, and I get to start school next year," Eve said.

She was eager to go to school, since her cousins started the previous fall. The twins were one year older and had told her stories about good teachers, recess, and pizza every Friday.

"I hope you get Mrs. Smith, she's nice, and her class always has parties," April exclaimed. "What are you gonna do for your birthday?"

"I think my mom is gonna barbecue. I don't know yet," Eve said.

Just then, Gia pushed her head out of the front door. "Eve, come on in here so I can braid your hair."

The little girl frowned, and the other two girls dropped their ropes to the ground. Juanita, the neighbor, walked past Gia and down the steps to the sidewalk. "OK, girl, I'll see you in the morning."

The short, thick woman walked past the girls, and her large hips rocked from side to side with an exaggerated motion that made her appear to be dancing. She had long braids with brown and honey-colored extensions that plopped down on her bottom with each bounce.

"See you later, guys," Jade said as she rose from the steps and followed her mother. "See ya," they all said in unison. All three girls walked into the house, and just as they were sitting down in the living room, they heard a knock at the door.

"Hey, hey, hey!" Uncle Mitch said.

He always smelled like motor oil from his work as an auto mechanic. The twins jumped up and hugged their father around his legs.

"There go my girls. Come on, we gotta get rolling. Thanks, Gia. We'll see you tomorrow," Mitch said.

"OK, Mitch, they already ate. You know which one didn't eat all of her food."

"Yeah, I know," he chuckled and closed the door behind them.

Eve sat on the floor in front of her mother as she braided her hair. They were watching a VHS tape of Lean on Me. Her mother was excited and pulled extra hard on her hair as she shouted her support of the school principal. "That's right! They ain't there to learn, so throw their asses out!" Gia loved movies with positive black male characters. The media showed so many examples of how black people did wrong in the world that she loved to see them doing something right, even on screen. Mr. Clark was a well-intentioned radical who went to jail for his controversial methods of eliminating drugs and improving the performance of the schoolchildren, largely of kids of low-income backgrounds. Eve grabbed onto the section of hair her mother was holding and pulled it toward her face. "Owww, Mom, you're hurting me!"

"Girl, sit still," Gia said. She couldn't understand how her daughter could be so tender headed, when she had braided her hair twice a week since she was about a year old. In fact, Gia thought she should be the one crying because the child's hair was so thick that her mother's fingers were always sore after she braided it. Gia worked through the tight curls until she made one ponytail with braids hanging off to one side of her head. Pretty barrettes in pink and white dangled at the end of each braid.

The little girl jumped up and stretched. Whenever her mother was braiding her hair, she would get so sleepy, but the moment her mother was finished, Eve's energy returned. She ran into the kitchen to grab an orange off the counter, and she bumped into her cousin Anita on the way.

"Watch where you going," the older girl snapped, punching her cousin in the shoulder. Anita wore a permanent scowl, and everything the child did seemed to annoy her.

"It was an accident," Eve cried.

She threw an angry glare back at her cousin and peeled the fruit. Anita sat down on the couch at the opposite end of her aunt. Gia switched channels. A different movie was playing, and this time Gia shed tears because a woman in the movie was having a breakdown over the death of her sick daughter.

Eve came back to the couch and sat flush against her mother's thigh. She leaned over and put her head on her mother's lap. Gia gently stroked the little girl's hair. She leaned down and kissed her daughter on the forehead.

"How about we take a trip next week for your birthday? We can go down to Baltimore and visit the aquarium. Wouldn't it be nice to spend the day down there?"

"Yeah, that will be fun. Have I ever been to Baltimore?"

Her mother thought for a second, then replied, "No. I haven't even been there since I was in my twenties."

Gia had grown up in Baltimore and left with Luther not long after they graduated from high school. He had gotten word from a friend that union work was available at a steel company in Wilmington. For almost two years, he had regular work and things were going well for them. Later, he was arrested for a DUI and lost his driver's license. Then, it became harder to get work, and he drank more and tried less.

"It'll be fun though," Gia continued. "I think you'll like it, and we can go to one of those places that have all-you-can-eat crabs and shrimp."

Eve became excited at the thought of it. The family often had a crab feast when there was enough money. Her father would steam them with beer, butter, and Old Bay seasoning. She looked over at her cousin and asked, "Are you gonna come, too, Nita?" The cousin rolled her eyes with disdain.

"No, I don't want to celebrate no five-year-old's birthday!"

Gia shook her head at her niece's bad attitude. "Oh yeah, because seventeen makes you grown right?"

The niece  clenched her jaw and kept her eyes straight ahead, only half-watching the movie. Through the corner of her eyes, she watched the mother and daughter, as Eve lay comfortably while her mother stroked her head lovingly. At times, Anita had tried braiding the little girl's hair, mimicking the aunt's actions. It never turned out quite right, and no one was ever impressed with her effort. Anita remembered Gia stroking her head and holding her the way she did Eve.

The teen ager dropped her head and blinked hard to keep back tears. So often, she had to hide the tears of jealousy and thoughts of the love she envied. Her little cousin had followed behind her since she was a baby. It wasn't until Eve was almost three that she could understand Anita was deliberately mean to her. Sometimes, Anita even felt bad when she went too far. She didn't like the person she had become and didn't want the child thinking of her as some sort of role model.

The older girl did her best to keep her little cousin at a distance, and her effort usually came across as pure cruelty. Several weeks before, when the child had asked for help getting a snack out of the cabinet, Anita had let go of her too soon, and the girl had hit her head on the kitchen counter. Anita was frightened because of the amount of blood that spewed from the wound. Even that night, the mother and father both coddled and kissed the girl so much that Anita couldn't help feeling robbed.

"I'll be back," Anita said, getting off the sofa. Gia watched her niece walk through the front door. Anita had been staying out late at night with a boyfriend she had on the west side of town. She was smoking weed and hanging out with a crowd of kids who made Gia cringe when they came around. She imagined most of them would end up dead or in jail. Many times, Gia had come home and scolded her niece for the smell of marijuana that met her at the door. Gia was saddened because she felt responsible for the change that had turned her sweet niece into this angry young woman.

The next morning, Gia called her daughter to wake up. She had poured a bowl of cereal for the girl to eat while her mother showered. Eve moved more quickly this morning than any other morning, excited about the day's events. When she finished, she ran back to the bedroom where her mother was getting dressed. Gia put a white princess dress on the little girl and a big white bow at the top of the ponytail she had made the night before. Even put on white socks with lace trim and white patent-leather shoes. Eve twirled around watching the edges of the dress flare up and down.

Gia was dressed in a beige dress and jacket ensemble and brown, leather, platform shoes. She had picked it up at a vendor's stall in the Farmer's Market where they have everything from electronics to the vegetables that she went to buy each week. It was pretty, and she thought she could wear it when she had something special to attend and needed to be a little dressed up. This morning, she decided the dress was the nicest thing that she owned for this particular occasion.

She threw a slate-blue, silk scarf around her neck and put on the earrings that Luther had given her for her fortieth birthday. She wore a cluster of silver bangles on her wrist and sprayed on her White Diamonds perfume. The dreadlocks she was growing curled under her ears and at the base of her neck. She had twisted them together and it gave them a wavy look. She loved her natural hair and vowed never to use chemicals again to straighten her hair. She never used them in her daughter's hair either.

"Oh mom, you look so nice! I want to wear that when I get married." The little girl marveled at her mother's beauty. There was one gray streak of hair at the very front and center of Gia's head, and it made her look even more beautiful.

"Thank you, Stinky. But I'm sure when you get married, you'll want a big wedding with a glamorous gown." She leaned over and kissed her daughter. When she exited the bathroom, the little girl was right at her heels.

Luther walked in wearing a pair of black dress pants, a white-collar shirt, and dark-blue patterned tie. "Wow, you look lovely," he said as he walked over to Gia and held her in his arms, kissing her softly on her lips.

Then, he lifted his daughter, "Look at my little princess. You're the prettiest girl in the world." The little girl tilted her head and smiled, showing the gap where her two front teeth had come out.

"Daddy," she giggled, giving him a kiss on his cheek.

Anita was still in the living room, lying on the pullout bed and pretending to be asleep. "Nita! You're not coming?" Gia asked. Anita lifted her head and shook it from side to side, then went back to pretending.

Outside the apartment, a crowd had gathered near several cars. They were all there to accompany them to the Justice of the Peace.

Uncle Mitch, Allison, April, Juanita, Jade, and several of Gia's work friends met the family on the sidewalk, greeting them with plenty of hugs and well wishes. Everyone took turns posing for pictures of the occasion.

Gia and Luther had been together for twenty-six years, and he finally asked her to marry him. She didn't answer right away and wasn't sure she would say yes. Actually, she wasn't sure he had really proposed. He had come in drunk one night, and she awoke to find him hanging halfway off the bed. She got up and began undressing him. He was too heavy for her to lift, so she straddled him to pull his shirt over his head. When his head fell back, his eyes were open, and he was staring into her brown eyes.

"Will you marry me?" he managed to ask her just before closing his eyes again, and snoring shortly after. The next morning, he said to her, "You never answered my question." Then, she realized his question the night before wasn't just the rambling of a drunk. They had been through so many trials over the years, and many of his actions hurt her deeply.

Ultimately, she decided that his sins were no greater than her own. It was not her place to be his judge. She thought of the good times. He had fostered her love of reading and encouraged her to keep her mind sharp and not just work herself to death. For hours, they would read about the antics of a Chester Himes' character and draw comparisons to the folks around them who shared some of the hilarious traits. The two of them had been together for so long, she was sure that she wouldn't be leaving him, and he wasn't going anywhere either. So she said yes, and they decided they would be married on a summer day at the county clerk's office.

Juanita looked over at the ground by the window. While the others were talking and laughing, she searched covertly, for an earring that she had lost the night before. Short on the money for her gas and electric bill, she had promised an ex-boyfriend that she would give him a blow job once a week for one month in exchange for the money. She was supposed to meet him the night before, but she was busy helping Gia to prepare food to serve after the ceremony. Before Juanita knew it, the time had come and gone, and she went home with her daughter. She would have just put it off for another day, but the selfish ex had called her home and threatened to tell her boyfriend about the deal they had made. So, she had let him come over last night.

Her boyfriend and daughter were in the house asleep. She didn't want to be too far away, so she had used the spot so many others did to do that sort of business. She sucked his dick fast and hard to get it over with quickly. Unfortunately, he wasn't the type of man to finish quickly. He purposely made loud noises and humped her face as her mouth made slurping sounds. Although her boyfriend could not hear them so many doors away, she feared her good friend and neighbor might. When she had finished, she tried to pull away, but he held her head tight while he ejaculated in her mouth. He squeezed her nose tight with his other hand forcing her to swallow his juices.

As she struggled to get free, the earring fell to the ground. When he let her go, he laughed as he zipped up his fly and whistled while walking off down the street. Juanita stood, adjusted her clothing, and looked up from the wall. Anita was standing there, watching her.

"Damn, Miss Juanita, I didn't know it was like that!" The unruly teenager wore a sinister grin and she said with a smirk. "Don't worry. I know how to keep a secret. I just want to be able to do it like you do one day."

"Yeah, I know you do!" Juanita replied.

Anita walked into the house laughing and shaking her head. Juanita went home without looking for the earring. She never liked having to make this arrangement, but for the first time she felt ashamed of what she was doing. She only had one more week to go on the deal, but she was sure he wouldn't let it end so easily, and she did not look forward to what he had in store for her.

"Juanita, come take these pictures for us, girl!" Gia yelled over to her girlfriend. She smiled, happy to have a friend in Juanita, who had always been there for her when she needed something. Juanita moved quickly to avoid drawing the others attention to the spot where her earring may be.

Luther picked up his daughter and posed for a picture with the two of them. They took two shots, one with a disposable camera and another with a Barbie camera that Eve had gotten as an early birthday present. Eve held on to her father's shoulder, smiling at Juanita who was acting like a professional photographer. Juanita stood on the stairs, and they looked up at her. Eve could see the curtain of the apartment window being pulled back. Standing at the window, her cousin Anita was staring at the girl and her father.

"Smile for the picture, baby girl," Luther said . The child leaned her head up to her father's and presented a wide gap-toothed smile.

After they took pictures, Eve's attention returned to the window, where Anita was still standing, and through the hazy film, she appeared to be crying. Eve didn't know why her cousin was so sad all of the time. Anita was often mean and hurtful toward her, but she realized her cousin was more sad than angry. The little girl mostly tried to stay out of Anita's way to avoid her wrath, but sometimes Eve wished she could help to make her cousin feel better. The curtain closed and Anita disappeared from view.

"Are you ready, sista-in-law?" Mitch said.

He had always liked Gia as a match for his brother. However, he knew she deserved so much better than Luther offered her. Before Mitch and Luther were separated as children, Luther had been the kind of big brother every little kid wanted. He was like a superhero, performing every task with ease, then step by step, teaching Mitch to ride a bike, catch a football, or string his fishing line. Mitch realized the pain of losing their parents was hard on Luther. It was hard on both of them. However, Mitch felt a little guilty when he thought of his brother's bitterness and anger. After all, Luther had to go to a home with no one there to love and guide him, while Mitch had a wonderful adopted mother and father who raised him as if he were their very own.

On many occasions, Gia would call him to

save her when alcohol fueled his brother's temper and some small offense on her part ignited his flame. Mitch had often prayed for his brother's sake that he would get his shit together before Gia came to her senses. If Mitch could have, he would have married her himself. Instead, he had impregnated a woman who loved to party, get drunk, and get high. Shortly after she had given birth, she left him, and he raised their twin girls by himself. As a result, he could appreciate a woman like Gia, who worked hard no matter what and stuck by her man.

Mitch smiled from ear to ear as he opened the car door for his brother with his wife-to-be and daughter. The twins sat up front of the Lincoln, looking back at them. From inside of the car, sitting between her mother and father, Eve looked out of the car window and could see the curtain pulled back again as the car drove away.

Luther looked from his daughter to his bride. Gia was the best woman, the best person, he had ever known. She had grown up in a middle-class, Baltimore family. Her father had sent her to private schools her entire life to keep her from falling in with the wrong crowd. He wasn't happy when he found out that the boy his daughter was dating was a ward of the state. He didn't care how well-read Luther was or that he was kind and polite. He didn't want any boy taking Gia's attention away from school, and he didn't think anyone was good enough for his little girl.

Gia and Luther met, however, at a museum where she had gone on a class field trip. Resident assistants at his group home had taken him there. His mother and father had died in a car crash that left Luther with only a few bumps and bruises. He was only twelve when the accident happened, and he had neither family nor friends to speak of. He became a ward of the state and lived in several foster homes temporarily. Then he went to a group home for teenagers.

His younger brother called and wrote often. Luckily, a good family adopted Mitch, and Luther didn't have to worry about him so much. On his first week at the group home, a girl named Rita befriended him, showed him around, and told him all he needed to know about living there. Luther told her all about his parents and the accident, and she continued to express interest in him.

She shared her own story with him. Rita was a rebellious teenager and her parents sent her to the group home because they could no longer control her actions and wanted her out of their house. Almost sixteen, she appeared much younger. She would sit with Luther at meals and hang out with him in the common areas throughout the day. She had a pale complexion with light-brown eyes and long wavy hair that she wore pinned up most of the time. When he turned thirteen, the staff threw a party for him, as they did with all of the boys, and Rita had danced with him the entire night. She made relocating there seem much more tolerable for him.

That night, after the party, they arranged to sneak out of their rooms after lights out and meet in a room that used for medical examinations. Luther had looked incessantly at the alarm clock waiting for the time to go by and bubbling with anticipation to know what his "first time" would be like. Rita and he had kissed many times, and he clumsily tossed his tongue around in her mouth. She was usually chewing gum, and sometimes, at the end of their slobbery exchanges, he would have the gum in his mouth.

The farthest he had gone before was placing his hand inside of her underwear and pushing his index finger inside of her warm wet privates. He was completely aroused by the look on her face as her eyes rolled in her head and then closed. He had moved the finger in and out quickly as he thought he should, but she grabbed his hand slowing his pace until he had the rhythm she needed. Finally, her body tensed and she grabbed her mouth and opened her eyes, tearing up as she climaxed and moisture enveloped his finger. Luther went the rest of that day without washing his hands. He had smelled that finger every chance he got, intoxicated by the aroma of her.

This night, when the clock read 11:30, he went to meet Rita in the sick room. He could see her sitting on the cot and looking over at the door. He smiled thinking she must have left her room early. He was carrying a book that he wanted her to read, and held it out toward her as he walked up. The book flew from his hand with a smack, and he felt someone grab him by both arms and cover his mouth. Rita began to let out a scream, but two boys that Luther recognized from the home muffled her as another two stood watching.

They tied Luther's hands behind his back and undressed the pair. They took turns fondling Rita and making her perform oral sex on Luther and kiss his feet as he sat there helpless to stop it. The other boys meant to degrade her. The last thing Luther wanted was to help them with their mission, but he couldn't quiet the erection in his pants. When one of them tried to force her onto the cot, Luther jumped up rushing him with his shoulders tilted, and the boy fell to the ground with a naked Luther falling on top of him.

"Get the fuck off me. What are you gay? Man, I think this dude is gay." the boy said. He looked at the others and brushed himself off as he stood up, leaving Luther lying on his side on the ground. Luther looked back at the cot, relieved that he had stopped them from hurting Rita. He was still looking at her as the boys huddled around something in the room and talked in a whisper. Luther began scanning their faces as they stood him up in front of the girl.

The one he had tackled stood in front of him pushing a finger in his face. "You trying to put your dick on me, faggot?"

Luther shook his head from side to side, knowing that they already knew that had not been his intention. They turned him toward the door in the opposite direction, and Luther could see one of the boys walking around him with a broom in his hand. Two boys flanked Luther, and he felt a hand grab his bottom. He began to struggle as he realized what they planned to do, and it took three of them to hold him down and keep him pinned to the ground. His screams were so loud that even through the gag someone pressed his hand over Luther's mouth to silence him. The assault seemed to go on forever as they pushed the wooden broom handle into his rectum over and over again.

Tears streamed down his face and snot dripped from his nose. When they were finished, the boys took turns urinating on him and kicking him while he lay still on the ground. Through it all, Luther could see Rita sitting in the same spot where she had been when he knocked the young thug away from her. She didn't move, she didn't speak, and she never lifted a finger to help him as he had done for her. After the boys left them alone in the room, he lay there looking up at her; silently he wished for death to take him away. Rita rose from the cot and walked in his direction. She looked down at his naked body, the mess that was all over the floor and the look in Luther's eyes. Then, she ran out of the room without even removing the ties from his hands. Help never came, and it didn't take long for him to realize Rita had abandoned him. Luther lay on that floor the whole night, thinking of ways he could die.

Someone from the cleaning staff found him there the next morning, and the administration rushed him to the hospital to get treatment for the wounds he suffered because of the attack. After several days, he came back to the home. Charges were filed against all four of the boys involved with the attack, and the administrators had them removed from the facility immediately. All of the other group home residents had heard of the ordeal, Luther assumed, through Rita. He was labeled a faggot and a snitch. The other residents ostracized him, and he had to look at Rita every day knowing she had witnessed his humiliation.

The museum trip came a year after the incident. That day in the museum, girls from the home and from Gia's school had exchanged insults because of some minor offense. He had watched from a distance as Gia played referee, trying to ensure that both sides were calm. She noticed him watching her and spent the rest of the day trailing him as he went from exhibit to exhibit. She asked many questions, stole occasional glances at Luther, and finally introduced herself.

She asked him why he wasn't hanging with the

members of his group, and he had said flatly, "I'm different."

"Me too," she replied, and she wrote her telephone number on his hand before running off.

He waited a month to call her, but each conversation with her was like a week's worth of therapy. They spent every moment they could together. When they were both finished with high school, he asked her to move away with him to start a life together, and she left everything behind to be with him.

On their wedding day, Gia and Luther stood in front of their guests and the magistrate of the court as he read the wedding vows. Gia looked into Luther's eyes. They were so different from the bright eyes of the man who had promised her they would be rich and happy. These were the eyes of a man who had been cast aside by destiny, beaten down by misfortune, and sealed his unhappiness with stupidity. She could see the gray outline that accompanied old eyes and the crow's feet that crept out onto his face as the years passed.

"For better or for worse, for richer or for poorer, in sickness and in health, till death do you part?" said the clerk. Everyone in the room stared at Gia, and the seconds seemed like an eternity. Yes, she thought to herself. "I do." she said.

Sorrow's Mate

# CHAPTER FOUR

Eve placed the last of her things into the suitcase she was packing. Just one semester after dropping out of her pre-med program, she was taking a trip to Costa Rica to shoot photos of volunteers teaching English to elementary school children. She had been doing well in her undergrad studies when, Jade, now a successful freelance writer, asked that she accompany her to Mexico for an article Jade was writing on international health-care access and affordability.

"You've been taking pictures our whole lives," said Jade. "I just need someone who can get me a few good shots to run with the article for this health journal."

Jade was right about the photos. Eve had received a camera as a birthday gift and got great joy from the images she captured on her adventures. The very first photo she took in Mexico was of a barefoot, little girl with big, green eyes playing in a puddle of dirty water and staring up at her. It had been a huge hit with the health journal.

Someone had described the photo as "Transporting viewers to the heart of the problem by emphasizing those most affected by the inequality in health care…the children."

Eve received requests from all over from others who wanted to use her photos from that trip. She also received many requests from others who wanted to have her take pictures for projects they had coming up. While she really enjoyed the work and the travel, Eve had not intended to launch a career at that point. After she left school, she traveled, mostly with Jade, and shot photos of whatever subject her friend happened to be covering.

Eve was going to enjoy this trip to Costa Rica thoroughly. She would be working for three days out of the twelve-day journey. She arranged for a tour that included hiking through the rainforest to the waterfalls and bathing in the hot springs of the volcanoes. She planned to go zip lining and white-water rafting if she had the time. That was what she had enjoyed most about the trip to Mexico, and what would ultimately help make the decision about whether to pursue a career as a professional photographer. She loved visiting new places and seeing how others lived.

On the day that she was leaving, Nathan would be working on a major project for a bank that wanted to build its headquarters in Delaware, so he would join her later. The bank wanted him to design a state-of-the-art building that would reflect their innovative approach to banking. He had figured out what he wanted to do long before she did. He was determined and finished his major in architecture in just three short years. He began working under a successful architect, Charles Todd. He grew up in the inner city and had a reputation for turning out great protégés, so Nathan had been fortunate to work at the company. It wasn't long before his hard work was recognized, and he took on bigger and more important projects, sometimes working side by side with Todd.

Nathan learned a great deal from the man, but it didn't take long for him to decide he wanted to venture out on his own and be his own boss. Steadfast and passionate about his work, he had remained persistent when door after door closed in his face. His first client was a real-estate developer who planned to build a mini mall in an underdeveloped area of the city. The neighborhood was starting to attract attention because of the new apartment buildings the developer was putting up. Nathan had done such a great job in planning the layout and coordinating with other engineers who worked on the project that he instantly made a name for himself. He breathed a sigh of relief after that because he wanted to take care of Eve, though she needed no one to take care of her.

Eve worked two jobs, one as an LPN -- she

had completed the program at Howard Vocational Technical High School -- and another bartending on weekends because she made good tips and could pick up additional hours as she needed without making any real commitment. All of this was while she worked on her pre-med program with the ultimate goal of becoming a family-practice doctor.

When she went to Nathan after the job offers began to roll in for photography, he simply said to her, "You do whatever makes you happy, and I'll take care of the rest."

She loved him for many reasons, but most of all he brought out the very best in her. He had kept in touch with her after he found her in that house. He was always asking her about school and things at home. She had gone to therapy for some time, and he used Emma's car to make sure that she got there and home safely. They never officially became girlfriend and boyfriend, but by the time she was graduating from high school, he was finishing college. He never had another relationship that she knew of in all that time. Eve had dated boys occasionally, but never developed enough trust to open up with anyone the way she had with Nathan.

The phone rang breaking her out of her thoughts. "Hello." The person on the other end sounded frantic and what they said startled Eve.

"I'll be right there!" she said, slamming down the phone, she grabbed her keys, and ran out of the apartment door. She didn't even close the windows she had opened or turn off the television. The elevator of her apartment building seemed to take forever going down four floors, and she pushed the button impatiently. When she got to the first floor, she took off running to her car and fumbled with the keys as she unlocked the door. The tires screeched, leaving a mark, no doubt, as she sped away. She raced through town, running several red lights and nearly hitting pedestrians who took their time sauntering across the road.

When she pulled up to her mother's house, she hardly came to a complete stop before jumping out and running toward the ambulance where Gia was being lifted inside on a stretcher. Her arm was bandaged and bloody, and she seemed disoriented and confused.

"Momma, I'm here. Momma, are you OK?" she yelled to her mom, pushing past the EMTs who tried to stop her. "I'm her daughter, I'm her daughter. I need to go with her."

With that, they let her by, and she jumped into the back of the ambulance and sat by her mother's side. As Gia awoke in the hospital bed, she seemed more relaxed than she had been the day before. She was extremely tired and her neck was stiff. Her eyes sagged with drowsiness brought on by all of the medication the staff had given her. She looked over and saw her daughter asleep in an armchair. A tray with cold eggs and pancakes was on the side table next to her. She was hungry, but she took her time forcing herself to eat the disgusting meal. She tried to move quietly to prevent abruptly waking her daughter. She also could feel the pain with every inch that she moved her arms. A dressing that covered them prevented her from seeing how bad the damage was. She couldn't remember anything, but she realized that she was in a hospital and in a tremendous amount of pain and that someone had injected her with something that made her fall asleep.

On her left side, an IV was hanging, with three different bags running into it. She presumed pain medication was in one of them because her body had felt much worse before. Just as she was finishing the food on the tray in front of her, a nurse walked in.

"Good morning, Mrs. Turner." I think it's time to change this bag. How do you feel, hun?" the thick nurse with the foreign accent asked with a smile.

"I've been better," Gia replied.

Her daughter roused from her position in the

chair, stretched, and then eyed her mother curiously. Eve had called Nathan to let him know what had happened and that she would be staying at the hospital overnight to make sure her mother was all right. He was very understanding and had even stopped to bring her dinner after he left work. He offered to spend the night, but she sent him home to get rest.

"I'll be back as soon as I can tomorrow," he promised.

Eve looked at her mother lying in bed watching the Maury Show on television the following afternoon. He was holding up a cue card and saying, "In the case of three-year-old Adrianna, you are NOT the father."

Two Hispanic guys sitting next to each other jumped up, clapping fives as they cheered. A white girl jumped up, ran off the stage, and threw herself onto a sofa that was in a small conference area backstage . Maury followed her, offering comfort in a hug and help finding the real father.

Gia shook her head in disgust.

"I don't know why these girls take themselves on this show and make a total damn ass of their selves. Those poor kids, not only do they not know their daddies, but the rest of the world knows how loose their mamas are."

"Mom," Eve said in the most non-confrontational tone she could muster. "What happened yesterday?"

Gia's facial expression changed. She wrinkled her forehead and raised one brow as she shook her head from side to side. She became very quiet and stared at nothing in particular. The day before, she had gone to volunteer at the soup kitchen, as she had done for months since retiring from the hospital. She came home and put some noodles on the stove for her dinner. The next thing she knew, some men were in her home grabbing her and attempting to take her out of her house. She had been so afraid of them, that she didn't notice the raging fire that surrounded them in the house. As she tried to dash away, she nearly walked into the inferno. Even the burn on her arms as they pulled her back did not register to her. She feared the strangers more than she did anything else, and she couldn't understand what they wanted from her. She didn't realize what had happened when Eve arrived at the ambulance and didn't recognize her daughter even as she sat there telling her "Everything will be OK, Momma."

It wasn't until that morning in the hospital, after she had awakened and began feeling the pain of the third degree burns on her arms, that she realized the severity of the situation. She became teary eyed and cried out, "Oh, Lord Jesus Christ, what did I do?"

Gia had worked hard for more than half of her life, saving her money. After her daughter moved out, she purchased the apartment building she had lived in for more than thirty years. She had enlisted the help of Mitch to find honest, hardworking men and paid them each week to come in and convert the two-apartment building back into a two-story row house. She had gotten a great sense of accomplishment with the purchase, and she even had someone knock down the wall next to the house to announce to the drug addicts and whores that her home was no longer their safe haven.

She had one of the young boys turn over the ground and advised him to be very careful, for there may have been countless needles in that dirt. He went to the Home Depot to purchase bags of soil and landscaping stones. One spring day, she went outside and planted a real garden. She had the frosted window replaced with a new one, and she placed a comfortable reclining chair in front of it, where she sat and looked out at her garden while she ate her breakfast in the mornings.

That night when she put the noodles on, she had forgotten them on the stove and her house had nearly burned to the ground, damaging the neighbor's home, as well. In the hospital, she was distraught and apologetic, and she explained to the doctors, as well as her daughter, that she had become increasingly more forgetful with each day. She told them stories of having found herself in familiar places at odd times, with no recollection of how, when, or how long she had been there.

After carefully examining her and conducting diagnostic testing, doctors explained to both Eve and Gia that she was suffering from early-onset Alzheimer's disease and that the progression had been extremely fast. The medical staff brought in images of Gia's brain with markers indicating areas of significant change to illustrate to them what was happening. Doctors explained that there was no cure and that they could only give her medication that might slow the disease process and prevent further degenerative damage.

The diagnosis shocked Eve so much that she called Nathan to come be with her at her mother's bedside. Before he arrived, Gia, having completely returned to her normal self, sat up straight and demanded that her daughter leave the hospital and go home to finish packing her things for her trip to Costa Rica the next day.

"You need to spend some time with that man before you head out," she said. "You don't want him looking for attention from nowhere else. He's a good boy."

Eve resisted, "Momma, I'm not going on that trip now. I'm gonna stay here and take care of you. Where are you gonna go when you leave here?"

The mother raised her voice at her daughter and pointed an accusing finger in her face. "Eve, I can take care of myself and have been long before you were even thought of. I don't need anybody fussing over me. Whatever needs to be done, will be done. Don't think you're gonna start treating me like some old cuckoo bird. I ain't dead yet!"

Eve flashed a weak smile and kissed her mother three times on her forehead "I love you lady," she said, before picking up her bag and walking out of the hospital room.

Nathan saw her standing outside the room talking to the nurse when he walked up. When she turned and saw Nathan approaching, she broke down into an uncontrollable fit of sobbing. She couldn't stop herself long enough to explain to him what was going on, so the nurse explained everything to him.

"Well, your mother insisted you go to Costa Rica, so that's what you should do. I'll check on her and make sure she is squared away before I come down to meet you."

Nathan went in without Eve to say hello to Gia, and she was happy to see him. He told her that he would be checking on her and asked if she needed anything.

"Just take care of that daughter of mine," Gia said. "Make sure she gets on that plane."

Eve continued to cry for forty-five minutes, and Nathan finally drove her back to their apartment. He finished packing her things and ran a hot bath for her, washing her like a baby and massaging her head until all of the tension melted away. He lifted her from the bathtub and dried her off on the bed, rubbing her down with body butter and brushing her hair and twisting two sections into a ponytail the way she did each night.

"Don't worry baby. Your mother's a fighter, and she'll be just fine," he said.

She thought to herself, "I have to remember to call Uncle Mitch in the morning."

Nathan made her a cup of chamomile tea, and she sipped it slowly while nodding off in his arms. When the alarm went off, Eve awoke to find Nathan standing over her handing her an outfit and kissing her face.

"I made you some oatmeal and cinnamon raisin toast, something quick," he said. "We should leave in about twenty minutes to make sure you're on time."

Eve didn't have time to protest; she was sure

that had been his plan. Before she knew it, she was sitting on a US Airways flight to Costa Rica. Jade would be waiting for her when she arrived.

Eve stared out of the window as the plane took off, and she closed her eyes as it ascended into the sky. When she opened them, she could see clouds floating beneath the plane's wings. She had been on airplanes many times, but the experience never failed to astonish her, looking down at the clouds that always seemed so far away from the ground.

So many things that seemed so far out of reach had come to her with little effort and a lot of good fortune, and just when it seemed things couldn't be better they had turned for the worse. She knew her mother would give her a hard time, but when she returned, she planned to lobby hard for Gia to come stay with her, where she could keep an eye on her. Her mother was everything to her.

Uncle Mitch had gone to check on Gia at the

hospital, but later that day he contacted the homeowner's insurance company and contractors to repair the damage to her home. She gave Mitch and Eve her power of attorney around the time that she retired, so he was able to make the necessary phone calls on her behalf. After his brother's death, he had taken on the role of pseudo-husband to Gia and father to Eve. When he took his girls anywhere, he took Eve with them and Gia also if she wanted to go.

He had watched Gia carry on with an amazing amount of fortitude with each tragedy that befell her. As the years went by, he had fallen in love with her. While she would never acknowledge any relationship publicly, in private they became closer than she had been even with her own husband. She had met Luther when she was young, before she knew who she was herself. By the time she realized that he was not the type of man suitable for the person she was becoming, they had already moved to Wilmington and gone through two miscarriages together.

Her father, a proud man who worked hard to support his wife and four children, had told her that if she left with that boy, she shouldn't bother coming back. The door would only swing one way. She never did. Her mother died first, and Gia grieved alone when her sister called to tell her the news. The fact that she never had a chance to say goodbye saddened her. Her father died a few years later of a heart attack or a broken heart because he had lost his wife and best friend of almost fifty years.

Luther had lost his family in a tragic accident, which began a succession of misfortunate events that left him more bitter and angry than the one before. She felt guilty at the thought of the happiness she felt being near his brother. She never slept with Mitch, but he sometimes held her in his arms until the early morning and tucked her in bed before going home. On several occasions, he had fallen asleep in the recliner and when he awoke, she had cooked him breakfast before sending him on his way. He gave her the type of love that Luther never could—an unconditional love that also provided safety and security.

Gia lay in the hospital bed thinking over the past few days. She finished eating the bland dinner and was not ready to fall asleep but also not interested in television or the magazines she had. The woman on the other side of the curtain was snoring loudly, but it didn't bother Gia because she was so lost in her own thoughts. The day before, she had been a very healthy woman, and for her age remarkably free of illnesses that plagued so many people in her community. While she was a very active woman, working hard at first at the hospital and volunteering there after retirement, she had experienced a great deal of stress for one person.

Working long and hard hours often meant that she didn't quite eat the way that she should have. Quick meals with processed or canned ingredients and fried food trumped a healthier option five out of seven days a week. If the doctors had told her it was high cholesterol or a resulting clogged artery that was ailing her, she wouldn't have been surprised. A diagnosis of diabetes wouldn't have surprised her either because high blood sugar ran in her family. Gia never expected, not in a million years, to hear that she was literally losing her mind. She had agreed to go into a rehab facility and then she would stay with Mitch until the restorations on her house were complete.

They were placing her on a medication called Aricept for the Alzheimer's. She wanted to go back home, to her house, but she realized that it was too dangerous for her to live alone. She thought about other people's accounts of her behavior, and she cried again at the thought that she did not recognize her own daughter. She had worked hard her entire life and been grateful for a body that held up with all of the wear and tear. She had never been seriously ill or taken medications, other than multivitamins, for anything. Her worse ailment had been her inability to carry so many pregnancies to term.

In the meantime, it was her mind that was sick, slowly stealing away the days of her life. She wondered what else she had forgotten and how long she had been forgetting. What precious memories, she wondered, were gone from her forever? She knew that many not-so-precious ones still burned deep inside of her mind. Just thinking of them, she considered that maybe Alzheimer's came with its own silver lining. Perhaps God had decided to have mercy on her, and instead of an early death or a long life full of regret and guilt, she would forget the love and the pain that she had experienced over a lifetime. She would look at loved ones like Eve and Mitch as total strangers, unable to recall the details of a beautiful birth or leisurely walk in the park. In addition, she would forget the feeling that overcame her when her daughter looked lovingly at photos of her father, missing a piece of herself. Gia hated the idea that she would be unable to care for herself because of the possibility of careless mistakes, like the one she had made at the stove. However, she welcomed a mind clear of hurt and a free conscience.

Sorrow's Mate

# CHAPTER FIVE

The room was dark, and Gia reached out but could not feel Luther in the bed next to her. She reached over to the side table and switched on the lamp. He had not come home yet. That was typical, since her husband had taken to staying out at bars late at night, drinking until he decided to come stumbling home. Though she was a married woman, Gia found herself alone in bed more often than not. She was so used to it that she would have been surprised to open her eyes and find him there.

It was still very dark outside and quiet, so she knew it was very early in the morning. She had gone to bed early and would probably be up longer trying to fall back to sleep than she would actually spend sleeping. Glancing over at the clock, she squinted to see the time, which read 4:15 a.m. Luther might not come home at all, she thought. She knew he had been seeing several women around the neighborhood. They had begun calling the house at times, cursing her, and telling her that he may be married to her but had been in their beds. Some had accused her of not knowing how to please her man, and one had even informed her that she was carrying his child.

"Honey, join the club," Gia said slamming the phone down on the receiver.

Later, Luther told her that the woman had an abortion, yet she was sure that he had his share of illegitimate children not far from home. He would stand at the door of the apartment talking to the women late at night. When she did say something to him about it, he would accuse her of trying to find reasons to get rid of him. Often, he would become violent; sometimes she would call Mitch to calm him down or take him out of the house until he sobered up.

Years ago, she had caught him standing down at the side of the wall with a woman, and argued with him because she couldn't believe that he didn't respect her enough to try to hide his affairs.

Really, she didn't care that Luther slept with

other women. She remembered her father taking her with him to the homes of women she called aunt. He would disappear behind a closed door and come back out with his clothes in disarray and sometimes a smudge of lipstick on his face or neck. Once, on one of his outings, he sat her down in a swing on a front porch. She had grown tired of waiting and crept quietly through the front door. She walked through a living room and then ducked behind a wall looking into the kitchen on the other side.

Her father stood in front of a woman with her dress hiked up in the front. His pants were down below his waist, and he was pushing himself into her while the woman quietly stroked his neck and back. Gia turned and moved so quickly out of the door that neither of them had seen her. Before they returned home, he would pick up whatever items her mother had requested from the store and remove any evidence from his face. He would walk into the house, always the loving husband, just in time with whatever item her mother requested.

Gia thought that all men cheat on their wives, but the good ones make sure their wives never find out about the infidelity and, of course, they never sleep with family members. Good men, even unfaithful ones, cared enough to take care of home.

Luther never learned that lesson. With any luck, he would leave her, and become someone else's burden. Lord knows, he had been hers long enough. She would never leave her husband, but she hoped that he would decide one day that he didn't want to come home ever again. Until then, she would carry out her wifely duties. She heard some movement in the living room. "I swear he better not wake that girl up!" she said aloud to herself. Gia got out of bed and threw her robe around her shoulders. She switched the lamp back off as she walked around to open the door to the bedroom. As she walked quietly up the hall, she thought she heard Luther whisper "Rita."

Anita had been out at the Club Millennium partying all night. She was staying with her on-and -off-again boyfriend she had met through one of her girlfriends from school, but they had argued the night before and when she returned to the apartment he had changed the locks. She stood there banging on the door and screaming for him to answer.

"Get the fuck out of here," he screamed back from the other side. "Go ahead and be a ho all your life!"

Her ride had already driven off and she had no phone and no money to call anyone to pick her up, so she would have to walk to the city. It was still mid-spring, and the temperature had not started to reflect the time of year. Tonight was very cool and wet with a slight mist in the air. She was chilly standing outside in a miniskirt and sleeveless silk blouse.

Before she left, she grabbed a bottle from the top of a trashcan outside the apartment building and smashed it against the sidewalk. She then wrapped a sweater she had been carrying around the top of it as she rammed the sharp edge into the tire of the ex-boyfriend's Acura. It took only two tries before the glass penetrated the thick rubber and air seeped out. Then she dragged the useless apartment key she was carrying along the side of the car as she walked off.

Drops of rain came faster, and she could feel them smack against her face. She thought of finding cover and waiting it out, but she didn't know how long she would have to wait. She decided to walk quickly and hoped to reach her destination before it got worse, instead of better. It was a very long walk, and she took off the heels she was wearing and walked barefoot, stepping in the grass and avoiding the glass and gravel that littered the side of the road when she could. She still had a key to her aunt's apartment, so she would let herself in and sleep on the pullout bed with her eleven-year-old cousin, Eve. In the morning, she would leave as soon as possible and try to get her things out of the apartment where she had been staying. She knew a girl in the leasing office who would let her into the apartment.

She walked down DuPont Highway and at that time of morning, many girls dressed a lot like her were out there. She looked at the women standing on the side of the road waiting for some strange man to pick them up. Many already appeared high off whatever drug moved them to stand there in the first place. The weather had no effect on them. Some of them stood posing almost like fashion models in the rain. A few of them didn't look that bad. When she walked close enough, they would speak to her: "Hey, honey," or "You got a cigarette I can borrow?"

For the most part, they seemed to be eagerly awaiting a customer, uninterested in anybody else's business on the street at that hour of the morning. Anita wondered if her mother had ended up out here or somewhere like it. Maybe she had gotten into the wrong car and her body had been dumped in some river or wooded area where they would never find her.

She looked over at a woman almost her complexion, and she could see her mouthing words into the air. The woman looked up and down the four-lane road then lifted her shirt and twirled in a circle. She did this several times, amusing herself more with each twirl. A bigger smile and heartier laugh accompanied each exaggerated motion. Anita was sure that the woman who was covered in red sores that dotted her arms, legs, and face and stood out against the pale skin had stepped into another body. She had become a ballet dancer, strong and defined, twirling on a stage in front of an audience. The smile on her face showed a person who had achieved a great accomplishment, and it almost made her look beautiful.

Then, it made Anita sad. Perhaps her mother was still out there, selling herself and forgetting the daughter she left behind years ago. Whenever thoughts such as those crossed her mind, she quickly formed alternative endings. No telling what had happened to her mother after she left her. For all she knew, maybe Jess had gotten herself together, married a nice man, and had other children. She was probably too embarrassed to say that she had gotten pregnant and left her baby, so she stayed away to avoid being reminded of her mistake.

Anita played out all of the different reasons why a mother might leave her child and never come back, some bad and others horrific. The worse the story, the better it made the girl feel because the thought of Jess living happily somewhere without her was too painful to bear. It didn't really matter what happened to her mother because it would never change what Anita had been in her life—a mistake, something to be forgotten or thrown out. She figured even a stray dog takes care of its young. So, Jess was no better than a dog to her daughter.

She thought back to that day at the abortion clinic, and it occurred to her that perhaps she was standing in a glass house. She didn't know what had caused her mother to run away, and the only thing she was sure of was that she would never find out. As all of these thoughts ran through her mind, a man pulled up to her in a blue Toyota Celica. He hit a small puddle that had formed in a little pothole, so mud and water splashed just above Anita's ankle. "Hey, baby, you going my way?" The man grinned from ear to ear, probably happy that he had found a hooker who had teeth and didn't look like she had been beaten most of her life.

"Yeah, if you're going to hell, motherfucker," she replied.

Anita learned long ago to be quick with insults, and she spat the words out in a way that made them sting. She leaned down bending at her knees to avoid showing what was under her skirt and wiped the mud and water from her legs.

"Fuck you, bitch!" He screeched off swerving a little as he made his way to the other side of the road to make a U-turn. He would undoubtedly go back and pick up one of the women he had passed the first time around.

Anita said to herself aloud "Nita, it's time to get your shit together. This shit is for the birds."

Later, after she retrieved her things, she would go down to Job Corps and sign up to start working toward her GED so that she could learn some kind of trade. She would also stop relying on men who sent her away as soon as they were through with her. She had been used all of her life and now she was finally tired.

She saw more of the same kind of women as she walked into the city, and she became a bit scared as she crossed the bridge at the overpass where the trains left the train station. She saw people sleeping on the ground, and she knew this was where the homeless congregated. They would go to a soup kitchen a few blocks away for meals. She picked up her steps and moved hurriedly across the road, eyes darting toward every moving thing in her view. When she turned onto the street where Gia lived, she uttered a sigh of relief. She hurried up the stairs and into the relative safety of the home where she had grown up.

Inside the apartment, Gia walked down the hall toward the living room and stopped dead in her tracks. Time stood still, and then it moved slowly frame by frame. She gasped and anger rose up in her chest as she stood again, staring at Luther's back. She ran at him in slow motion, fist clenched, punching him in his neck and back. Luther raised himself up from the pullout bed, where she could see Eve still asleep. Luther punched Gia's face so hard, she fell back against the wall and hit the back of her head. Sound in her ears turned off, except for the blood she could hear rushing through her head. She lifted herself up and backed into the kitchen as he walked slowly toward her. She looked from him to the girl, trying to calm herself and keep quiet to prevent her daughter from waking up. Gia took deep breaths, slowing the movement of her chest and steadying the wobble in her knees. Eve had not stirred. Gia hoped the girl had remained unharmed. Luther also looked over at the girl. Lust had been replaced by the look of fear on his face. Fear that he would not be forgiven for this latest transgression. He whispered, "Gia, calm down! This is not what you think." His eyes told the truth, though his mouth continued the lie.

"Yes, like Anita?" she whispered, and the words cut him deep, so he furrowed his brow and his eyes narrowed to small slits on his face where only the black of his pupils were visible. She ran into the counter behind her with no place else to turn. She quickly grabbed a knife from the dish drainer on the counter. Luther reeked of alcohol, and his eyes were wild and bloodshot. She didn't know if he was under the influence of any other drugs and she didn't bother to ask. She knew he had dabbled in heroin a few years back but didn't think he used it regularly.

Her heart raced in her chest, and she opened her mouth to make a plea to her husband. "If you leave now, I won't call the police on you."

After several seconds, Luther's wild eyes grew redder and seemed to glow. She begged him, "Luther, please."

Almost crying now, her hands began to shake uncontrollably, including the one holding the knife. She tried to steady them, but it was too late, he noticed her unsteady hands, and she could see that he realized she would not stab him. She had told him often enough "I love you, I'll never hurt you."

Luther knew that he could trust those promises made with the purest intentions from the kindest woman he knew. She had forgiven a million offenses and stayed loving him harder each time. He knew that her hope was for him to become a better man, one who did not test the bounds of her love so regularly. No matter what he did in that moment, Gia would remain with him until the day she died. He was the only man she had ever been with and the only man she ever would have.

"You're not gonna do nothing baby. You'll never hurt me, remember," he said.

The fear intensified in her eyes, and he could see that her mind raced to figure out what she could do next. With that thought, he lunged toward her quickly and lost his footing on the kitchen floor mat. He slipped and fell forward, and the momentum drove his head onto the sharp corner of the kitchen counter then down onto the vinyl floor. He lay there in a daze but conscious as blood flowed from the gash on his head.

Gia ran back over to the pullout bed where her daughter remained sound asleep. Gia did not stop to check his wound or look back to see if he rose from the floor. Eve's underpants were down around her thighs, exposing her privates, but Gia saw no visible indication that she had been touched or penetrated. Luther's head had been so close to the girl that Gia thought his mouth was touching the daughter's tender flesh. Gia pulled up the panties and threw a blanket over her small frame. Eve drew her legs up to her knees and sighed deeply, but did not wake from her sleep.

Gia had always fussed with the child to get her up in the morning, but had never been happier that she was a heavy sleeper. She looked at her daughter sleeping peacefully, and it reminded her of the day she had found Luther with her niece. Anita had been only a year older than Eve was now, and she had been naïve enough to believe at least half of what Luther said when he accused the girl of coming on to him. She had continued to care for Anita, but not the same way she had. The child had grown into a woman without the benefit of unconditional love, and it was no fault of her own. Just then, Anita walked through the door and straight into the kitchen.

"Oh, my God, he's having a seizure," she

screamed.

She ran for the phone and picked it up. It wasn't until Gia snatched the phone from her niece's hand that the aunt realized she was still holding the knife. Anita looked at her alarmed and afraid. Gia tossed the knife down and whispered, "He tried to do it again."

Anita was puzzled. She didn't understand at first, but she looked over at the pullout bed and saw her baby cousin lying there with the blanket partially covering her lower body.

"He tried to do it to Eve," Gia said calmly placing the phone back on the receiver. The two women turned to look at the man lying on the kitchen floor. He had caused them both so much pain. Anita cried, as she watched Luther twitch and convulse involuntarily. She looked back over at the young girl and wondered if he had actually done it. She wanted to know if Luther had done the same thing to his own daughter that he had done to her. Was this the first time or was it already too late. She would ask Eve if anyone had ever touched her, or hurt her in any way.

Meanwhile, Gia looked into his eyes and at his outstretched arms. Blood still flowed from the wound, and frothy saliva spilled over his lips as he mouthed,     "Help me."

She didn't move or lift a finger, and she still held the hand Anita had picked up the phone with tightly. The niece looked back and forth between the injured man and her auntie, the glue that held their family together. What she saw in Gia's eyes was not the anger or evil glare of a murderer. What she saw was a woman who was simply tired. One who had come home one too many nights to a man that burdened her with an increasing load of despair. Gia was going to let Luther die, to rid herself of the burden.

Anita wanted to call 911 to have someone come and help him. She would take Eve out of the house herself if Gia refused to report the sexual abuse to the authorities, but she didn't want to stand by and let him die. He was, in fact, dying right there on the floor in front of them, in a spot where he had even taken her at times.

She looked back to her aunt and said with pleading eyes, "You can't just let him die?"

Gia watched as Luther struggled to hold on to life. He tried to turn himself over, but he had no strength and finally the struggle ended. Gia took a deep breath and looked at her niece, the one she had been too stunned or too stupid to protect so many years ago, and said, "Till death do us part."

Eve cried uncontrollably at her father's funeral. He was after all her first love. She looked around the room at all the sad faces around her. Her mother was sitting straight up wearing an all-black dress with black high heels and sunshades that were so dark no one could see her eyes. Her Uncle Mitch sobbed quietly, and on either side of him were his daughters holding his hands. Men her father had worked with over the years were at the funeral. Neighbors came by to pay their respects. Members of the church Gia began attending showed up in large numbers to give their condolences. People had brought food to the house every day since the news of Luther's death a week ago. Gia was glad to have the gifts because she didn't feel like cooking. Several women were there whom Gia didn't recognize, and each one cried almost as hard as she did as if they were his wives and not her. The one person who was absent at the funeral was Anita.

The morning Luther died, Eve's mother woke her early and handed her long pajama pants and a lightweight coat. She saw melancholy on each face, as she looked around confused. "What's going on Momma?" Gia looked into her eyes. "There has been a terrible accident, I need you to go over to Miss Nita's, and I'll come explain everything to you in a little while," she said. She had gotten up and put the clothing on as instructed, and Miss Juanita stood at the doorway waiting to take her over to her house.

As she walked past her mother and cousin, whom she could tell had been crying, Eve noticed something on the kitchen floor. She could make out a person, and she moved quickly in that direction.

"Daddy?"

She ran toward the kitchen and Gia attempted to grab her, but she was too late.

Eve dropped down on her knees beside her father's lifeless body screaming, "Oh, my God, somebody help him, somebody help."

Where Eve had kneeled was a small pool of Luther's blood, and it stained the pajama pants. She grabbed his face, kissed him, and called out, "Daddy, get up! Please, Daddy!"

Gia cried for the first and only time over Luther's death because she could feel her daughter's pain. She turned and looked away. Anita walked toward her cousin and reached down to touch her shoulders, but Eve turned and screamed, "Don't touch me! What did you do to him? You killed him! You killed him!"

Anita's mouth dropped open. This time, she was the injured one after an altercation with Eve. She was hurt, and although she understood the girl's pain, Anita wanted to tell Eve that she had been spared from becoming another one of her father's victims. She wanted to tell her that he was a mean drunk and that he would force himself onto her friends, as he had done with her, until the word got out, and she had none left. Anita wanted to tell Eve that she did not kill him, but they let him die to make sure that he would never harm his own flesh and blood. She had so much she wanted to say, but she kept quiet, knowing now was not the right time. Eve kept shouting, "You killed him," pointing her finger in her cousin's face.

Gia grabbed Eve by the shoulders and declared, "It was an accident baby! He was drunk and fell down and hit his head."

Eve's body shook, overwhelmed with sadness at the loss of her dad. It had been easy for Juanita to pull her along and lay her in Jade's bed to rest after removing the soiled pajamas. She stayed there all day. Eve lay in her best friend's bed quiet, grieving and refused to go home that night or the next day. As she lay there, she replayed the scene in her head repeatedly. She remembered seeing a knife on the ground after her mother woke her and thinking it was odd.

Anita's face had appeared riddled with guilt,

and Eve was sure that it was because her cousin had played a role in Luther's death. Her cousin had always hated them. She hated them all. Eve was angry with her mother for allowing Anita to continue coming and going from their house. Anita had made it clear that she hated them, so why was her mother always bending over backward for her. Eve thought that by holding onto Anita, Gia was holding on to her own sister Jessica, whom she hadn't seen since she ran away. Gia had filed a missing person's report and run ads in local papers with the photo years ago, but no calls ever came. This evil likeness was all that her mother had left of her sister, and holding on to that memory had destroyed their family forever. Eve was sure that her mother had lied to protect her niece, and she was sure that Anita had killed her father.

# CHAPTER SIX

It had been several months since her father's death, and Eve sat in front of their living room window reading the last book he had given her as a gift. A girl named Nicole in her English class who was new to the school took a seat next to Eve. A copy of the same book was among the things she placed on the desk in front of her. It wasn't until then, that Eve remembered her father had left Their Eyes Were Watching God on the counter for her the day before he died. She had intended to start reading it sooner, but her devastating loss made it hard to concentrate.

"Do you like that book?" she asked Nicole.

"It's all right," Nicole answered. "I was reading it for a book report before I left my other school, so I figured I'd finish it in case I had to do one here."

Now, Eve was almost in tears as she realized that Janie would lose the love of her life. The woman went through so much to find someone who finally made life worth living, just to lose him.

Eve wondered why Zora Neale Hurston had chosen that way and that place for him to die. Eve thought a man like Tea Cake should have died a more dignified death. He had spent his life loving Janie and trying hard to make her happy. He was unlike the husband with whom Janie wasted the first part of her life, the one who had been able to die with the respect of the townspeople.

As Eve read on, she also became angry with Janie for returning to the town. Had she not learned anything? The man she loved died trying to show her that life was more than the house, money, and good reputation she left behind. Why go back? Now, his death was also in vain. Janie would live out her days in a house that had been more like a prison than a home and that carried reminders of a loveless relationship, and not sweet memories of a passionate romance.

Luther had told Eve that she would love the book, and he had been right. He was right most of the time about her taste in books and art. He knew her and though both of her parents valued education, her father had really valued beautiful things. He would walk past a field or down a concrete sidewalk and notice a lone flower that had managed to bloom with no one to care for it.

She had just returned to school and it was a relief to have something to occupy her time. She had spent the entire summer agonizing over memories of bicycle rides, cookouts, and day trips with her dad to the surrounding states where they would visit historical sites and interesting places. Her father wanted her to learn as much as she could.

"So you don't ever have to break your back to live," he said. "You have to use your mind."

She missed him so much. Her mother was wonderful, but Eve had spent so much of her childhood at home with her father while Gia worked that he had become his daughter's very best friend. He would play wonderful jazz that she had grown to love over the years. He told her that Gia and he probably conceived her on a winter day to the sounds of jazz music.

She walked over to the radio that sat on the kitchen counter and grabbed the cassettes that were next to it, flipping through them until she found the one she wanted. The white label read, "My Favorite Things -Coltrane." It was her mother's favorite, and her father would often play the music as she walked through the door from work. He would meet Gia at the door and hold onto her arms and then dance with her until the weight of the world had eased off the woman's shoulders. The song would play for thirteen minutes, and then they would finally stop dancing, and Luther would kiss her and say, "Hello."

Eve would watch in awe of the love between the two of them. Even Anita played the song occasionally when the two cousins were alone in the house, and she too would seem a little less angry at the world. A few times, Eve remembered her cousin grabbing her the way Luther would and rocking her back and forth in her arms.

He had made such an impact on them all, and Eve missed him more every day that went by. She hoped that one day she would find a man who would care enough to lift the weight of the world off her whenever he saw it breaking her down.

She slipped the cassette into the player and the song began. Immediately, Anita's stomach turned, and she yelled to her cousin, "Turn that shit off, you see me watching TV." Anita avoided anything that reminded her of Luther, especially during the day when she could control it.

At night, he visited in her dreams. Sometimes she was a little girl, and he was there again, making her feel like the luckiest girl in the world. In some of them, she called him Dad, but all the dreams led to Luther dying right in front of her eyes. At times, she would be making love to him, and then the blood would appear on his forehead or his body would shake as it did that day on the floor. Thoughts of him evoked feelings of guilt, regret, but mostly shame. She couldn't bear to listen to that music.

Gia sat at the small, square table where they ate their meals. Across from her, Juanita was holding her hand of cards while they played Tonk.

She stopped long enough to scold her niece,

"Don't talk like that in here."

Gia, on the other hand, had not thought much of Luther since his death. She loved him, but the moment he took his last breath, a calm had come after a lifetime of storms. She didn't know if she was in the eye of the hurricane, but she planned to enjoy the beautiful weather and didn't think about what might await her on the other side.

Periodically, Anita looked over at her cousin. When Eve caught her looking, she would suck her teeth or roll her eyes. Nonetheless, Anita wanted to ask Eve something. It was something Anita had wanted to know so badly that she had been at the house every day, not looking for anyplace else to go.

She had started at the Job Corps, received her high-school diploma, and begun working on a medical billing and coding certification. She was doing much better, and even her attitude had improved. But there was still something that bothered her. Every night before she went to sleep, she prayed about it and hoped that her cousin would not turn out as she had. Anita realized that all of these years she was trying not to be close to anyone, especially not Eve. Anita wished she had talked to Eve, taught her about people, and the way the world worked.

The moment Anita saw her young cousin lying on that bed, she regretted not taking the opportunity to be a more positive force in her life. Anita figured once the girl could walk and speak for herself, nothing was left for her to do. She had played the secret guardian long enough, and besides, the little girl loved her father, and he seemed to love her, too. Had his love transformed from that of an adoring protector into something twisted?

Gia and her friend were laughing hysterically now. The topic had turned to the newest neighbor, who had moved into the apartment were Juanita once lived with Jade. Juanita had applied for and received a public-housing unit, and Jade had transferred to a school outside of the city. Many landlords came and went over the years

The new tenant had five children by several

fathers. "Girl, not one of them damn kids look alike, and they don't look like the ones they calling daddy either, if you ask me," Juanita said.

Gia laughed at her friend, who may have come by to play cards or have a drink, but her favorite pastime was gossiping about someone else's business.

"These girls are a trip, out here spitting out a bunch of community babies!"

Gia wrinkled up her nose and repeated, "Community baby?"

Juanita looked at her incredulously, "Mmm, hmmm! Those babies belong to everybody honey. Everybody done put a little bit into them."

They both laughed at the ridiculous notion and continued their card game.

Anita was sitting on the new futon that Eve used as her bed, watching a rerun of Family Matters on television. Anita turned to face the pair at the table and began to laugh. Gia looked at her niece with a half-smile, wondering what it was that had tickled her so.

Anita stopped laughing abruptly. "What was

that, Miss Juanita? Everybody put a little bit in huh?" Anita inquired with a sarcastic smirk.

She waited for an answer, but Juanita remained quiet and returned her attention to the card game.

Anita had seen her on more than one occasion right outside the apartment performing favors for men other than her live-in boyfriend. The last time, a man had been standing behind her with her dress raised and panties down. He was humping her from behind, and she threw her wide behind back at him, making him moan with delight. When they finished, Anita pushed her head over the stair railing to get a better look at the man, wondering if he was the one Juanita saw so often after that first time. Word had spread that Juanita would perform favors when she was in a bind, and many were willing to pay to play.

The man standing there that evening bent his head down to fix his clothes and remained pressed back against the wall in the shadows. When he stepped out into the open where the streetlights dimly illuminated his face, Anita gasped in horror at what she saw. Her heart began to pound on her chest, and the two heard her and looked up to find her watching them. Luther wore the familiar grin and shrugged his shoulders as he walked off down the street carrying a bottle.

"Anita, please you have to understand...," Juanita began to explain, begging her not to tell Gia.

Anita had rolled her eyes at the explanation and simply said, "I'm not what you have to worry about Miss Juanita. Karma is a bitch."

She turned and left the woman standing there like an admonished child. The next few times they had all been together, Juanita looked at her suspiciously, no doubt wondering if the girl had kept her secret. Their encounter had been a few months before Luther's death, and Anita was sure Juanita had already breathed a sigh of relief.

She often listened to her talk about other people, including Camille, the young woman who moved into her old place. Anita had befriended the woman, and sometimes would babysit for her when Camille couldn't find anyone else. She was a white lady who had grown up in New Castle. Going to school with a mixed population of city and suburban kids, she had grown fond of the white 'hood boys. The more tattoos and worse the attitude, the more she liked them.

The fact was Camille did have five different children who had five different fathers. Her own father had molested her, and she was thrown out onto the street before her seventeenth birthday. A story would begin with each man she thought was the one and end with a child. Night after night, one man after another made his bed at the apartment with the woman and her children. Each one forgot her as they left and moved on with their lives. The white men  would come looking for her in the neighborhood, standing out among the many brown faces.

The children shared their mother's blond hair and brown eyes. She took very good care of her children, and two of the fathers were somewhat involved in their kid's life. One worked as an auto mechanic and made sure Camille always had a running vehicle to commute safely back and forth.

Another had become a real-estate and insurance agent who made good commission. He provided child support, and the family could call on him when they had no food or a bill was past due.

The others were thugs or losers whose main interest was sex and who had little or no interest in anything else. All of them had moved on to relationships with other women they treated much better than they did Camille. With each one, she suffered a blow to her self-esteem that made her allow the next man to treat her with even less respect in the hope that he would stay with her.

Anita didn't care about Camille's ways, and maybe it was because she carried her own share of skeletons. She shared some of those with the two women sitting in front of her. She had found a kindred spirit in Camille and sitting there listening to Gia laugh as Juanita criticized her made her angry enough to let Karma have its day.

"It's funny you mention everybody putting a little bit in," Anita said. "I was wondering, since Luther's dead and gone, who else has been putting a little in you?"

Juanita's dark face went pale as all of the blood rushed away from it, and she stood straight up. Gia and Eve both stared at Anita with a question behind their eyes.

Eve spoke first. "What are you talking about?"

She grew angry at the audacity of Anita, mentioning her father's name in such a disrespectful way. Gia turned her attention to Juanita. The affair with Luther had been no affair at all. It was simple blackmail. Like Anita, he had seen her down there on many occasions, making ends meet, as she liked to call it. Luther had been fresh with her before, but she knew well how to shrug off the advances of a drunk. Once, he had found her with a man other than her own, and Luther's advances became much more aggressive. One night, as they passed each other in the vestibule outside of the apartment door, he stumbled into her. When she moved to walk away, he pushed his body up against hers, grabbed her crotch, and firmly squeezed it.

When she opened her mouth, he covered it with his other hand and whispered, "You better shut your mouth, unless you want me to head right over to your house and tell what I've seen with my own two eyes."

He removed his hand from over her mouth, and Juanita stood there letting him grope her. He pulled his member from his pants and told her, "Touch it."

She had placed her hands around it, and he grabbed it, motioning for her to move it up and down on the shaft. She did it quickly, looking back at the door, praying that Gia would not hear them and come to see what was going on. After he ejaculated onto her hand, he took some of the thick liquid, rubbed it onto her face, and laughed.

"I can't wait to see you again, Nita," he said as he walked into the apartment without looking back.

Now, Gia's friend stood there staring at her. Overcome with guilt, Juanita ran out of the apartment to her car. Gia heard the engine start and the car pull away. She stood up and turned to walk down the hall toward her bedroom.

"You're a lying little bitch!" Eve screamed at

her cousin. "You hated my daddy. You always hated my daddy. He's dead, and now you want to try to drag his name through the dirt!"

Anita's eyes never left Gia, who looked on without saying a word as her daughter chastised the cousin.

Anita said to Eve, "Your daddy had more dirt on him than you could ever know, baby girl, and your mother's not so clean herself."

She turned to make eye contact with Gia. "Am I a liar, Auntie?"

Anita stared hard, as her aunt's eyes looked back and forth between them. The niece was waiting for Gia to respond and needing very much to hear what her answer would be.

"Am I a liar, Auntie?" she asked her again.

This time, Gia could hear the pleading in Anita's voice as it cracked and as the tears began to run down her face. Gia looked at her niece. She realized what Anita was asking her, and that the question had come from another time and place altogether. Gia looked back at her daughter, so angry and protective of the father that she had only known as a man who loved his family.

Not wanting to hurt either of them, she simply said, "We all have our sins."

Anita did not realize how angry she had been with her aunt. The young woman knew how hurt she was by her aunt's reluctance to call Luther what he was, and to say finally that the niece had not been responsible for what went on between them. Yet it wasn't until she had jumped off the futon and knocked Gia to the floor that she realized she was still fuming with anger. She thought that some parts of her past had been buried with the man so instrumental in shaping the person she had become, and that those things had no place in her present or her future. The aunt who had allowed a man to die to protect her own daughter had also allowed her niece to grow up in a house with a man who molested her.

Anita yelled, "Tell her!"

Perhaps Eve needed to be cautioned by the truth and not protected from it. She should know that danger could be as close as the room down the hall.

Luther had come over to Juanita's one day to pick up Anita during the summer before Gia came home from work. Her aunt had made provisions to keep the two of them apart while she was not at home. Anita knew she wasn't supposed to leave with him, but she did not want to refuse and cause a scene.

Back at their apartment, the ugly Luther reared his head. He called her names like "little whore" and "fast-ass little girl" while he raped her brutally. By the time Gia came home, Luther had left the apartment. Anita lay there on the bed bloody and bruised from the assault. Gia washed and dressed her before putting the girl back in bed. She never asked or cared to know what had happened. Anita was sure that she knew, that Juanita had told her Luther picked her up that day.

At that moment, thinking back on that day, the anger rose up to the surface and Anita could not control it. She grabbed her aunt by a handful of the dreads that fell onto her shoulders and hit her repeatedly. The snap and jerking of Gia's head as her niece's fist connected with her face made Eve cringe.

Anita screamed at Gia as she hit her, "What were my sins. What were my sins? You are a liar. You're the liar. Tell the truth."

The niece raised her fist in the air staring with furious eyes at her aunt's battered and bloody face. As Anita was about to bring her fist down once more, she heard a deep gasp, and the room went silent. Confusion showed on both their faces, then the air seeped out of Anita slowly and her grip on the locks released. Her big, brown eyes were wide now, like a deer caught in headlights. She coughed softly, and Gia could see blood splatter from her mouth and pool at the corners of her lips. Anita dropped down to the floor, and her aunt caught her in her arms.

Standing there looking down at them, Eve cried quietly. The knife, dripping with blood, was still in her hand, by her side. Gia stroked her niece's face and pressed her hand against the spot on her back where the blood was expanding across her shirt.

She was speaking to Anita, "It's OK, baby! We're gonna get help. Hold on Nita, hold on. Eve, call 911."

She looked up at her daughter and then back to her niece, who was crying and looking at her, fear had replaced anger in her eyes.

"Hold on baby, hold on."

She screamed at the daughter who had not moved, "Eve, call 911!" She screamed again, "Eve!"

She realized her daughter was in shock and she laid her niece down to run to the phone. It took just a few seconds to tell the woman at the other end what was happening. Someone had stabbed her niece, and she needed an ambulance right away. She gave the woman the address and returned to Anita's side.

The young woman was coughing violently, choking on the blood that pooled out of her mouth now. She mouthed, "Auntie" in a barely audible tone.

"That's right baby. Auntie is here. Auntie has always been right here. I love you, and you're gonna be just fine. You know that. Who loves you?"

Gia rocked the girl as she had done hundreds of times before and kissed her on her blood-smeared cheeks. Anita's fingers wrapped around her aunt's hand with no force behind them. Anita's grip grew weaker within seconds as the last of the air seeped out, and she was quiet and still.

Gia let out a deafening scream, "Nooooo! Nooooo! What have you done?" She said rocking back and forth with her lifeless niece in her arms. "Oh, Lord, what have you done?"

She looked down at the last of her sister that remained with her and cried harder. Holding Anita, she felt as though she had been the one holding the knife, and that she had killed her long before that day . The guilt stopped her from fighting back. Guilt reasoned that this was the price she must pay, and now it was time for her take her punishment. She never saw her daughter grab the knife, or she would have stopped her. Gia would have let Anita continue to batter her face as penance for what she had allowed to happen.

Looking up briefly at the girl holding the knife, she screamed again, "What have you done?"

Eve opened her mouth but no words came out. She had been angry with her cousin for what she had said about her father. She hated Anita because her cousin hated Luther. Yet what drove her at the moment she grabbed the knife was not anger.

She had been screaming, "Stop! Stop," as Anita was hitting her mother, but the look on her cousin's face made it clear she did not intend to stop and could not stop herself if she wanted to.

Eve thought of the father's funeral again. She thought of herself at another funeral, this time her mother's. Eve saw that vision so clearly and again the only person missing was her cousin. Eve thought about the night that her father died again. Anita had been standing there with eyes swollen and red, and her mother was trying to send Eve away to prevent her from seeing his body, his skull cracked open as he lay out on the kitchen floor. Eve believed that Anita had killed her father, and that was the thought as she picked up the knife.

She had yelled at the cousin's back, "Stop it, Nita! You're gonna kill her!"

The way her cousin had raised her fist so high above her mother's already bloody face, she knew she had to do something. The knife was already in her hand. It seemed as if she was moving in slow motion when she pushed it into the soft flesh, and finally her cousin had stopped. Now, her mother was looking at her, hurt, crying, and asking her what she had done.

"I killed her," Eve said.

The confession fell from her tongue as heavy as concrete, and she turned and ran out of the house and kept running. She never stopped until she reached a bench in the park where her father had often taken her. She sat on the bench until it got dark. The events of the day had been like a nightmare. She had had nightmares like that before. She had awakened some nights out of bed, because they had been so real. Sometimes, she would awake as a child and think that she saw her father standing there staring down at Anita and her as they slept. She would squint in the dark, trying to adjust her eyes to the light. When she did, he would be gone. One night, she asked her father if he was in fact standing by the bed the night before, and he told her "No, that was a nightmare, baby girl."

In the darkness, she walked off into the wooded area so that the park rangers, or anyone else for that matter, wouldn't find her. Her eyes were open wide. The sound of every cricket chirping, bird screeching, and the rustling of leaves was like a bullhorn in her ears. She stayed very still until the morning when she moved deeper into the woods to be out of site from the path for runners. Time moved slowly, and the day got brighter and warmer. Then, the sun disappeared and the night would grow cooler. All sorts of thoughts went through her mind. She had killed someone, and when the police found her, they would take her to jail. What would become of her there?

Her mother was angry, and surely, she wouldn't want to speak to her. Eve thought about Anita. Why had she been so angry? Why couldn't she just sit there and watch the TV, or leave like she always did when she got mad. Why did she have to start an argument?

Eve stayed in the park for as long as she could until her stomach ached so badly that she thought she would die. She didn't want to die there, where no one would find her. So, she came out of the woods and walked away from the park.

# CHAPTER SEVEN

Gia was beside herself with grief. She had put off planning the funeral services for her niece, because she was going out of her mind in search of her daughter. Gia hadn't seen Eve go out the front door. She had been hysterical, and it took more than an hour for emergency response officers to calm her down. It took another hour for evaluation of the wounds to her face and hand.

Then, the police took her to the local precinct for questioning. They had expected her to claim that she stabbed her niece in self-defense, but the wound on Anita's back and Gia's injuries were consistent with her story that her young daughter, shorter in stature than Gia, had stabbed the cousin.

The question now was where was her daughter? Gia didn't realize Eve wasn't with her until she began telling the police details of the events. They had contacted all of the friends and family that Eve might turn to, and no one knew where she was. Toward the end of the third day she was missing, the telephone began to ring. Gia stared at it for several seconds, afraid of what might be in store for her. In a few short months, she had lost two people very dear to her, and the one left was somewhere alone in the world. Her worst fear was that Eve would never return to her, and as with her own sister, she would never find out what happened.

"Hello?" The woman at the other end spoke slowly in a Southern accent, "Hello, may I speak with Gia Turner, please?"

"This is Gia," she replied.

"Gia, my name is Emma Monroe, and I think I have something that belongs to you."

Emma spent an hour with her on the phone, and Gia poured out her heart to the woman she barely knew who was taking care of her daughter. Emma told her most of what happened with Eve, but spared the details of the near rape the girl had experienced. From the sounds of Gia's story, she had already suffered enough.

Emma, Nathan, and Eve drove to Gia's apartment, where they all sat and talked as though it was a normal visit between friends. When day turned to night and the conversation died down, Emma walked over to the girl and kissed her forehead.

Then she leaned in close to her and whispered, "The road you traveled on yesterday doesn't have to be the road you take tomorrow."

Eve looked at her and understood exactly what Emma was trying to say. The girl wrapped her arms around the woman and smelled the scent of the Avon body cream Emma had given her after her shower. She held on tight to Emma, and thought this is what it must feel like to have a grandmother.

Over the next few weeks, Gia and Eve spent time at the police station talking to officers about what had happened the night Anita died. Eve told the truth, but the detail that worked in her favor was the battered face of her mother. Since she was a minor and had acted in defense of her mother, they would not charge her. A judge ordered her to undergo psychiatric counseling, beginning with a 30-day detention during which a specialist would evaluate her and recommend whether the court should release her. She would be at the Rockford Psychiatric Center. Eve was twelve but was in a group that had children as old as seventeen. She took part in group sessions several times a day. Some of them she found helpful, and others she felt were useless. She learned to talk through her problems and to address the things that bothered her. She told the staff and group members how much she actually loved her cousin, and how she had always hoped they would grow up to be more like sisters. The most important thing she learned was that nothing she had been through could compare to the ordeals of some other patients. She forgave Anita, and she forgave herself.

In the meantime, Gia, with the little money she had, arranged for a small funeral service for Anita. Many young people came, most in their early twenties. Gia recognized some of the ones whom Anita had brought around, but she had never seen most of them. Groups of young people wore T-shirts with the slogan "RIP Nita" and photos of her niece printed on them.

Juanita was at the service right by her side, holding her hand. Her friend had even picked out clothes for Anita and viewed her body at the funeral home before the service to make sure that everything was right. Juanita was a good friend, and despite what she had done, she had kept their secret for over a decade. Anita was in a different cemetery from Luther's. Gia thought that the niece deserved some peace in the afterlife, especially since she had never gotten it in the flesh.

After thirty days, the court released Eve into the care of her mother, and they took their time rebuilding their life together.

Gia had grown less resilient over the years. Her outward smile could no longer tell a lie. Anyone looking at her could see that she had experienced a great deal of pain in her life. She only made any real effort where Eve was concerned. The dreads grew wild and unkempt on her head, and she slept most of the time. She would be in bed whenever she did not have to work. The house became a pigsty. Eve would try her best to keep things in order, but she focused most of her energy on making sure that her mother ate and washed herself every day.

After listening to some of the testimonies at the Rockford Center, she watched Gia carefully, looking for signs that her mother might harm herself. Daily, Eve asked her questions such as "Am I gonna see you when I get home?"

She surveyed the home for any sharp objects, medication bottles, alcohol, and anything else she thought could be a potential threat. One night, Gia didn't come home and Eve waited up all night. When the sun came up with still no sign of her, Eve called Nathan and Miss Emma. By the time Gia showed up later that day, Miss Emma had cleaned the apartment from top to bottom, and cooked a meal that made them feel like they were eating in a five-star restaurant.

Gia was still wearing the clothes she wore to work the previous day, and her hair was somewhat disheveled and her eyes were swollen, red, and crusty. Miss Emma had taken her to the bathroom after spoon feeding her for more than an hour and run Gia a hot bath. Miss Emma stayed in the bathroom with Gia, and when they emerged, Gia was clean and her locks were pulled back into a ponytail. Eve watched Miss Emma walk her across the hall and close the bedroom door behind them.

After about fifteen minutes, Miss Emma emerged and said to Eve, "Let your mother get some rest. I'll be over in the morning to get you off to school."

Every day for almost a year Miss Emma came to the house, cooking, cleaning, and talking with the two women. Eve didn't know if it was the food, the clean house, or the conversation, but something in the two of them seemed to come back to life during that year. Gia emerged from the cocoon in which she had closed herself up, and she became a beautiful butterfly, loving her daughter harder and harder with each day that passed. Gia found a good friend in Miss Emma, and often invited Nathan and her over for dinner or cookouts in the summer. Gia talked with Eve about love and the importance of finding joy in one's life.

"You are my joy," she said, "but there is joy to be found in all the wonders of life. People will come into your life and leave, but the joy that they bring in the time they are there is what you have to hold onto."

Eve was happy to have her spirited mother back, this new Gia, one who worried less about overtime and time-and-a-half. Life for them settled into a new normal that was an improvement over the way things were before.

In school, Eve worked hard and participated in the drama club, dance troop, and cross-country track team. Her laid-back demeanor and friendliness toward everyone made her increasingly popular as the years passed. She and Nathan spent a lot of time together as well, since he would accompany Miss Emma to the house almost every day. He helped Eve with her homework and drove her to places where she could take pictures.

He never took advantage of her or let on that he liked her in a romantic way until she was close to graduating from high school. One day, he was looking through her photos as they all sat around in Gia's apartment. Things had gotten much better there, so Miss Emma and Nathan visited less often. This time, they hadn't seen each other in more than a week. Miss Emma and Gia were catching up, and Gia was explaining her plans for renovating the house that she purchased from the landlord.

Nathan stopped at one particular photo, staring at it very intently. Eve had gotten an expensive new camera as a seventeenth birthday gift, and one of the very first photos she took was of herself, using the timer mechanism. When she walked over and looked down at him, the picture of her was the one at the top of the pile. He looked up at her strangely and said in a soft whisper, "You really are beautiful."

Still, they continued hanging out and just being friends. They would go to movies, college homecomings, and theater shows when he found something that interested them both. Nathan was a lot like her father in the way he valued education and learning about cultural things. Though she would never say it aloud, Nathan was in many ways better than her father. He did not drink alcohol, smoke, or do any type of drugs.

Nathan never got into fights or arguments with anyone. He got along fine with everyone, including her Uncle Mitch, who gave him "the talk" when they finally began dating . The twins had moved away to school, sharing a college dorm room. Uncle Mitch had bought a house in Middletown but he visited often and made sure that Eve and Gia had everything they needed.

Nathan was there for Eve for whatever she needed. One day, in her freshman year of college, they sat outside of her dorm, eating ice cream and talking. Eve leaned over to wipe chocolate syrup from the corner of his mouth. As he laughed at himself for being so clumsy, his huge dimples and bright smile made her want to kiss him. She leaned in close and kissed him long and hard, placing her hand behind his neck. He had been reluctant at first, but soon began to return her affection. When they separated, he studied her face. Smiling and nodding his head, he said aloud, "Yeah…OK."

One day a year later, he asked her to go with him to New York to see The Lion King on Broadway at the Minskoff theater. They took the train and then a cab and checked into the Crowne Plaza hotel in Times Square. They walked the streets, enjoying the sights and sounds of the energetic city. He took her shopping for a nice dress, although she didn't think she needed to get dressed up for the evening. She purchased a low-cut, fitted, pink dress that was cut on an angle just below the knee and slanted down to a point at the back of her calves. He bought her a pair of shoes with silver straps.

Eve loved the musical. She had seen the Disney-animated movie many times as a child and could sing along to the songs. The props and effects were amazing. She felt as though she could see birds flying high above an African plain, while zebras, giraffes, elephants, and lions bowed and raised themselves on hind legs to show their respect to the little prince.

Several times throughout the show, Eve became giddy with excitement; and each time she laughed, she caught Nathan staring at her. She looked at him inquisitively, and he would just look away. She began to wonder what was on his mind. After they left the theater, she rambled on about how fantastic the production was and how she wanted to see more Broadway shows. "Huh," Nathan said looking back at her.

They walked side by side, and Eve stopped with both hands on her hips. She had grown into quite an attractive young lady, and the dress hugged her rounded breasts and thick thighs.

The fabric drooped at the neck and Nathan could see the tops of her plump breasts.

"Nathan! Eve yelled. She had been asking him when they were going to come back to New York City, but he hadn't heard a word she'd said to him. "What is going on?"

He walked up to her and stopped to lean in a

little and touch his nose to hers.

"You're absolutely beautiful. You are my very best friend. I don't know why God chose me, but I am so thankful he did. I want to spend the rest of my life with you, whether that's one day or sixty-five years."

He bent down on one knee in front of her right there in Times Square  as people brushed past on either side of them, and a crowd gathered around them, cheering him on.

 "I've been trying to think of the best time and the best way to ask you this question, and every moment with you seems like the perfect moment. Will you do me the honor of being my wife?"

He pulled a small, black box from his pocket and opened it, displaying a simple, gold engagement ring with 2 karat diamond. Her eyes welled up with tears, and Eve began to shake as she nodded her head up and down. She knew that something was strange about Nathan's behavior lately but had never expected him to propose. In fact, she had spent little-to-no time thinking of marriage. His words moved her beyond measure, and she felt a flutter in her heart the moment his eyes softened and he reached his hand out for her to take it.

The crowd that had gathered cheered and applauded them as Nathan stood up and scooped her up in his arms, kissing her passionately. Their story had been no fairy tale, but it would have a happy ending after all, she thought.

That night, they had returned to the hotel and had dinner at the restaurant in the lobby. Most of the time, they stared at each other and laughed like a pair of high school students on a first date. They explained to the waiter that they had just become engaged. The restaurant treated them to a bottle of champagne and large piece of triple-chocolate cake to share. Nathan picked up the strawberry on top of the cake and reached across the table toward her. Instead of taking it from his hand, she pushed her lips up against it, opening her mouth slowly. Then she bit into the fruit, before running her tongue along her top lip sensually, never taking her eyes off her fiancé.

Nathan tilted his head to the side. He had

never seen this side of Eve, and he was enjoying the show. Under the table, his pants bulged in the front, and he covered his lap with his napkin to avoid any embarrassment.

"Let's go upstairs," she whispered softly.

He moved so quickly, that she laughed at his eagerness, before rising out of her chair as he pulled it back from the table. They walked hand in hand to the elevator. As they waited to ride up, Eve playfully leaned with her backside against him, rubbing up against the hardening lump in his pants. When the elevator came and the doors closed, she turned to face him and kissed him with one hand around his neck while the other caressed the throbbing erection. A beep notified them that they had arrived at their floor, and the doors opened. Just as she turned around, a group of women stood staring into the elevator car, waiting to step on.

Eve pulled Nathan by the hand behind her down the hall, and the minute they were inside of their room, she unfastened the pink dress and let it drop to the floor, and stepped out of it. The king-sized bed had a white leather, upholstered headboard and a blue paisley duvet.

She slowly removed the white bra and matching thong underwear she had on, bending over in front of him as she pulled them to the floor. Her full calves flexed in the heels, which she kept on even as she turned around to sit on the bed.

"Come here," she commanded, moving her index finger in a back and forth motion.

He obeyed and walked right up to her, and she wasted no time unfastening his belt and zipper. She kissed the curve of his hips and pulled his thick penis from his underwear. She stroked it with her hands as she looked into his eyes, then took it into her mouth and began mimicking the women in the porn movies she had seen. She sucked in her cheeks and bobbed her head up and down. Her right hand wrapped around the shaft and moved up and down with her lips. He moaned more and more the deeper she took him, and the excitement made her convulse between her legs. Taking too much, she gagged and had to hold her mouth to avoid vomiting the delicious meal they eaten downstairs.

He removed the rest of his clothing and climbed into bed next to her. He traced the curves of her body with his fingers, kissing her slowly with his mouth slightly open so that there was a wet trail that went from her toes up to her pussy area. He played with the most sensitive part of her anatomy, sucking and teasing it as she writhed in ecstasy on the bed. He took a finger and rubbed her clit back and forth, and when he saw that she was climaxing, he pushed it inside of her causing her whole body to shutter and stiffen before relaxing again. He moved up until they were face to face.

He positioned himself to go inside of her, and she said, "I've never done it before."

"I know," he said.

Nathan took his time making love to the woman who would be his wife. When he could no longer hold back, he erupted inside of her.

They lay there afterward, talking about anything, everything, and nothing until he was aroused once again, and she welcomed him into her arms.

# CHAPTER EIGHT

The baby was born on a hot summer day. She came rushing into the world, as if there was something she needed to do that couldn't wait. That's the way Eve would be into her adulthood. Gia and Luther were not prepared for the baby because they had been too preoccupied with everything else happening around them. Gia took a paid maternity leave for eight weeks from the hospital. When it was time for Gia to return to work, Anita volunteered to stop at the Kuumba Day Care Center and pick up her baby cousin on the way to Juanita's house. The center was only a couple of blocks from the house. The staff was composed of mostly young black girls and a few older black women. The sign on the door read: "Grow healthy hearts and minds."

It had a rainbow-colored jungle gym, protected by a big, red fence. She longed to see the baby play out there on the slides and swings. Her cousin did absolutely nothing but eat and sleep. As for the day-care center growing health hearts and minds, the staff simply placed the babies into beds and let them sleep or lie there as long as they didn't cry. Still, Gia felt comfort in knowing the center had enough eyes around that the baby would be safer than she would in the care of someone alone at home. Gia had agreed that it was a good idea for Anita to pick her up, and it would save them money on the hourly day-care fees. She would keep a close eye on the baby, even as Juanita and others fussed over her.

At home, Anita would change the baby's diapers the minute she soiled them if Gia were busy with something else, and she would change any clothing that was wet with the baby's drool or milk from a leaking bottle.

Luther gave Anita mean glances, and at one point snapped at her, "She's my damn daughter!"

His wife's niece didn't know how deep the sickness in him ran. She couldn't imagine any father who would desire his own child, but she would not leave the helpless infant to fend for herself. Day in and day out, she kept a watchful eye, even as the relationship between father and daughter began to grow. It wasn't until Eve was almost three years old that she began to follow her big cousin around less and the father around more. By the time she was four, she had become daddy's little girl, and still, Anita would accompany them on park trips and outings because trust was not a luxury she could afford.

Around that time, Eve had begun falling asleep in the bed with her cousin at night and wanted to stay there through the night. Gia agreed that it was a good idea for her to sleep with her cousin, so that Luther and she could have their bed to themselves again. Anita stayed awake most nights, and when she did sleep, it was with one eye open. She had looked into the innocent brown eyes and seen something precious worth protecting.

Legally, at the age of sixteen she could have left the home forever. She could have gone away and never seen Luther again, but she stayed to make sure that the innocence remained unblemished. She adored the little girl with big brown eyes like her own, but Anita was also sad and afraid for what life would have in store for her. She had seen firsthand how life could steal the joy that came with childhood ignorance.

She thought back to the day she asked for the Popsicle and remembered how she had looked up to her uncle. She had wished often that he were her dad. In many ways, he was like a father to her, and a lover as well. Before he changed their relationship forever, she had been the child he showered with books, trips, and affection. He had been more nurturing than Gia, who was too tired most of the time to go anywhere except work. When she fell while learning to ride a bike, Uncle Luther had picked her up and dressed the scraped skin with a Band-Aid. Luther had taken her back outside that same day and set her back on her bicycle, despite her protests. He told her to hold on to the handlebars.

"Trust me," he said. "Uncle Luther isn't gonna let you go."

She pedaled with all her might and began to smile, realizing she was almost doing it all by herself.

When she called aloud, "You see me riding, Uncle Luther?" she realized from his distant voice that she was indeed doing it all by yourself.

"I see you baby girl," he shouted at her back.

She stopped and then pushed back on the pedals, putting her feet down on the ground. She jumped off the bike and started running back toward her uncle's outstretched arms, and then leapt into them. It was as though he had taught her how to fly. Every day with him had been like that until that day she had the Popsicle. That day, he clipped her wings and she never left the ground again. She had held him in very high regard, although she knew how alcohol changed him, and she had witnessed many fights between her auntie and him. She had simply shrugged off each fight, thinking, "Uncle Luther's drunk again."

It wasn't until Uncle Luther's demons became her own that she knew alcohol was only where the sickness began. It ran through him, pulsing through his veins with the very blood that sustained him. The sickness was so much a part of Luther that without it, she was sure he would die, as he would if he lost too much blood.

On Eve's fifth birthday, they all took a trip to Baltimore and spent the day walking along the Inner Harbor. Her aunt and uncle had just gotten married the week before, and in public, they resembled happy newlyweds, holding hands and kissing each other every opportunity they could. They had gone to the aquarium, and even she started to believe in the role she played in this happy family. That day she was the beloved older cousin, lifting the girl to show her the exhibits she was too small to view. They laughed together as they ran their hands along glass windows with small sharks, starfish, and coral in the tanks. They took pictures of themselves standing next to huge glass windows where larger fish swam as freely as they would in the ocean.

The girls were amazed at everything they saw. Eve begged to have her face painted, and when she was done, she asked her father to take a picture of the three women. Anita, Gia, and Eve posed in a warm embrace and smiled. Yes, this looked and felt much like a real family. They found a restaurant with an all-you-can-eat seafood buffet , and the four of them devoured piles of crabs, shrimp, and crawfish. When they finished, their bellies were full, and it began to get dark outside.

Before they returned to the car, Luther ran off to grab something from a store. They were waiting when he returned, and he removed a small paper bag from his pocket, untwisting the cap from whatever was inside.

Gia said, "Luther, can't you wait until we get home."

He ignored her protest, but the change in attitude showed on his face . The ride home was quiet, and he didn't appear to be driving impaired at all. He emptied the bottle of liquor sip by sip as Gia cut her eyes at him the entire trip home.

As soon as they entered the apartment, the argument ensued. Whenever Luther drank, they would argue. Often they did it in front of the two girls but most of the arguing took place behind a closed door that did not keep all of the scathing words from floating out.

Anita had gone into the room one day and said to them aloud, "She can hear you. We can both hear you out there!"

They had been arguing about how he behaved in front of the children, and Luther said something to Gia that Anita feared Eve would hear. She was not only there to protect her from inappropriate touches or kisses, but she would have to protect the girl from words as well. Words could do far more damage in a much shorter amount of time. Her fear was that the damage would go unnoticed. They would yell and scream and their venomous insults would fly beyond the barrier and strike the child. Neither mother nor father, both too angry to notice or care, offered consolation.

Anita had witnessed this many times herself. She hoped for her cousin's sake that Eve would make it through her childhood believing she had a mother and father full of love and affection, and not two people so flawed that they clung to each other to fill the holes that were missing within them. After Anita brought it to their attention that Eve and she could hear them, the two made an effort to quiet their voices when they got into altercations, or Luther would simply walk out and visit with one of his concubines around the way.

Once, when the ladies had gone out to run errands, they found Luther and some work buddies in the apartment upon their return. At the sight of the beer cans, liquor bottles, and a powdered substance that she thought was cocaine on the dinner table, Gia sent the girls back out. Luther and Gia started arguing, and the other men scattered.

Anita had taken Eve to Juanita's, but returned and stood outside of the door. Luther was sky high, with snot running from his nose and saliva from his mouth. He also reeked of alcohol. Gia was hysterical and visibly shaken by his state of intemperance. She begged that he leave and get himself together.

"Look at you, Luther, your killing yourself!" Gia said. "Do you want your daughter to see you like this? Please go get help. I'll call around and find a place for you to go, and I'll take you myself."

He was quiet as she made her plea, but then from outside the door, Anita could hear things slamming and smashing against surfaces. She ran into the room to find Luther holding Gia down on top of the table , and bottles that had once been there strewn about the room.

"You think I'm some impotent nigga you can just command as you please," he hollered. "Why, because you went to some private school and your parents were all high and mighty? Look at you now! Look at you now! I'm not going a goddamn place! If you want to take them kids and leave, ya'll go 'head. I don't need you."

Anita ran toward the two. She picked up a bottle off the floor, and as Luther held her aunt down screaming into her face, she cracked him over the head with it. He fell to the floor still conscious, but disoriented. Gia jumped up, grabbed the niece by the arm, and they left together going to Juanita's house.

Gia called Mitch and he showed up shortly afterward and went into the apartment to get his brother. After some commotion, Mitch was able to overpower Luther. Mitch yelled insults laced with declarations of undying love.

Those were followed by hardened threats, "If you ever put your hands on her again, I'll kill you myself. If you ever bring that shit in this house again, I'll kill you myself," Mitch assured his older brother.

Mitch continued his threats as he placed Luther into his car and drove down the street. Gia went back to the apartment, and Anita soon followed her. When she walked in, her aunt was bending over, picking up the litter from the floor. Although Gia was still very strong, she looked much older to Anita than just a few years before.

Anita blamed her aunt for the part she played in the way things had unfolded, but the niece knew that it had hurt her aunt deeply as well. Anita couldn't imagine watching someone you love behave the way Luther did, and always leaving the mess for her aunt to clean up.

Anita went into the kitchen, grabbed another trash bag, and started at the other side of the room. Neither of them spoke a word, and every once in a while she stole a glance at Gia. The girl was thankful that Aunt Gia was not a different kind of person. The niece knew her aunt could have thrown her out on the streets when she found Luther and her in her bed. Gia had tried, what she felt was her best, to protect her.

Now, Anita picked up the last of the glass on her side of the room, and she began to hear what sounded like a light grumble and grow louder and louder. Gia was still staring down at a bottle in her hand, and the tears poured down her face.

"God, give me the strength," she repeated. She looked up as if she could see through the tattered ceiling right up into heaven and begged, "Please, God, give me the strength."

Anita felt sorry for Gia, but she thought changing her situation could be as simple as leaving him. Gia worked hard enough. She didn't need the burden his constant screw-ups caused.

"You're better off without him," Anita said.

Gia looked at her niece, and she stopped her prayer for just a moment. She glanced at Anita for a moment, and then she spoke up to heaven again, "Give me the strength to carry out your will."

That night, as the girls lay asleep in the living room, Eve asked Anita, "What was wrong with my daddy?"

Eve hadn't said much when they brought her back home. She did ask where her father had gone, but no one gave her an answer. Noticing something was wrong, she remained quiet and obedient through dinner, her bath, and finally at bedtime.

Anita looked into the innocent eyes and said, "He was tired."

Eve had a puzzled expression on her face, but the little girl didn't ask any more questions. The cousin grabbed her and pulled her close, holding her in her arms. "You are so special, and don't ever let anybody tell you any different. Where you come from doesn't change who you are."

They sat silently staring at each other for several minutes.

"Anita," Eve spoke in a low whisper, "Can I be your friend?"

Anita smiled at the baby girl. Tears formed in her eyes, and the trust and respect the little girl offered in the question moved her. Not wanting to have that burden, to have the potential of disappointing, she removed her arms from around her and pushed her to the other side of the bed.

"We don't need to be friends. We're cousins."

For five days, Mitch stayed at home with his brother. He strapped Luther down to a bed using leather belts linked together around his arms and legs. He refused to let him go until the toxins left his body. Mitch had called around to different places that offered detox services, but they needed the intake to be voluntary, and many required insurance or payment that Mitch couldn't afford. He put his brother in his daughters' bedroom and took the twins to Gia's to stay for a few nights. They told the girls it was like a sleep over. Their excitement thwarted any questions about why Uncle Luther was staying at their house.

The next afternoon, Luther began to break out in sweat, his nose ran profusely, and he cried, begging his brother to free him. That lasted into the second evening.

"Mitch, man, I'm dying. Mitch, I need to get out of here man. Help!" He screamed.

At one point, Mitch walked into the room and nearly fainted from the overpowering, noxious odor of urine and feces. He went to the bathroom and retrieved towels, wash clothes, and a basin. He filled the basin with soap and water and placed it at his brother's bedside.

"Do you remember when we were kids?" Luther said. "We had some good times didn't we, Mitch? Let me go, man, I'm gonna die in here. Do you want me to die like this? I can't die like this Mitch."

The two brothers became separated when Luther was twelve and Mitch was eight. At first, they went to different foster homes. Mitch ended up with a nice family. The father was a Baltimore police officer, and the mother was a homemaker. They decided to adopt him to ensure he stayed with them. They explained to Mitch that they would never try to replace his parents. He kept a family photo of his parents with their two boys, which he still had to this day. His brother had not been as lucky after the accident. Luther had gone from one foster home to another until he ended up in a group home. He stayed there until he graduated from high school and then took off.

Their mother and father were both working-class Southerners from Mississippi who migrated north looking for better wages and opportunity. Their father found work at Sparrows Point steel mill in Baltimore, and their mother was a sanitation worker at Johns Hopkins Hospital. Their father instilled in his two sons the value of hard work and the idea that little else mattered in the world.

One day as they were all on their way to a grocery store, a drunk driver hit their parents' car, causing it to flip over several times. When help arrived, both their mother and father were already dead. Neither boy sustained any life-threatening injury, but the accident altered their lives forever. Mitch felt he had lost both parents and his fun-loving big brother that day. They kept in touch over the years and stayed close to each other because they were all they had left of their family.

"I'm not gonna let you die, Luther. That's why you are here, man," Mitch said. "I'm trying to help you live."

Sorrow's Mate

# CHAPTER NINE

The disease progressed quickly, manifesting itself more and more as the seasons changed. On several occasions, Gia had been confused, hungry, and disheveled when someone came by. Mitch decided to move in with her to keep an eye on her. At first, it had worked out. He had been there to redirect her and calm her down. They spent days taking walks and he read to her. They spent hours reminiscing on good times and changes for the worse.

They spoke of the neighborhood that had deteriorated so much that they were afraid to speak to anyone without hesitation and they placed bars over the windows and dead-bolt locks on the doors to keep out unwanted company.

"These folks around here are out of control," he said.

It seemed Mitch's very presence kept Gia more oriented, and they both were happy to have the company.

Although his mind was sharp, Mitch's body was beginning to break down with old age. He filled his pill case each week with eight medications for a list of ailments, including hypertension and diabetes. His vision worsened due to diabetic retinopathy, and severe arthritis made it difficult for him to walk. Even in his condition, poor Mitch had been reduced to tears on many occasions when Gia, confused, had accused him of hiding women in the closet of the house.

She had even pointed out the window at women who walked by declaring, "There she is. That's the one right there."

He begged Eve to believe him that those things weren't true. Eve knew that it was the illness causing her mother's accusations. She had been the victim of them herself. Gia accused her daughter of stealing money that they later found tucked away in her brassiere, folded inside a small wallet, or rolled up in a handkerchief.

One morning, Mitch had awakened to find that Gia was no longer in the apartment. He took his time creeping up and down the surrounding blocks looking for her in familiar places.

"Gia! Gia, honey, where are you?" he called out into the open air.

He went back to the apartment, out of breath and fatigued, and called Eve to come help. They contacted the police, who sent out an automated phone alert to the area residents. It notified them that an elderly woman was missing from her home and gave Gia's description. It gave the date and time she was last seen, which had only been the night before. By early afternoon, they had received a phone call and a city police officer had picked up the sixty-six-year-old woman, dressed in only a nightgown, extremely confused and afraid. She did not recognize Eve or Mitch, and had to take the sedative Ativan to calm down.

By three o'clock, she was back at home and in familiar surroundings with the people she loved. Gia was back to being herself. They recalled to her vivid details of her behavior and told her how they found her wandering outside. She agreed that Mitch was no longer able to take care of her and that they would go into a long-term care facility. She refused to be a burden to her daughter, who had so much living left to do. Gia and Mitch moved together into the Frenchtown Manor assisted-living facility. It was a lovely place, and Eve paid what Mitch and Gia's retirement benefits did not cover. They sold both of their homes, liquidated assets, and put the funds in an account for their additional needs.

Every two months, Eve arranged a trip and took her mother away for a few days just to spend time together. For their last outing, they visited a bed-and-breakfast in Cape May, New Jersey, but Gia had been more confused than she was lucid while they were there. So the trips stopped six months before Eve's wedding, but she hoped that her mother would be present in mind and body when it came time for the nuptials.

Back at the facility, Gia was sitting alone in the dayroom of the living facility. She had a television in the small apartment that she and Mitch shared, but she liked to watch the people come and go. The dayroom was a large, open room with huge bay windows. On one side was an electronic, sliding glass door that allowed the residents who were able to scan a bracelet to go out and sit down at the patio tables there. Since Gia was often confused, her bracelet would not open the doors. If she got too close to them when they were open, an alarm would alert the staff that she might be wandering away.

Still, she liked to sit there and look at the purple and white garden outside the doors. The men who worked outside mowing, weeding, and trimming the grounds would wave at Gia as they passed by the windows. She had tried to make her garden as beautiful as this one, and though the flowers were never so full and the blooms not quite as bright, she missed her own little garden.

Almost four decades of her life had been spent behind the same walls and it was more time than she had spent living any place else. She thought of the elderly couple in her old neighborhood that had refused to sell when the management company offered them money. Gia agreed with the other neighbors back then, that if she'd gotten the same offer, she would have sold without any hesitation. Now, as she sat in the facility where she would live out the rest of her days, she understood why the couple had refused. If you spend enough time in a place and with a person, they become a part of you, and it's hard to part with a piece of yourself. She often talked with the staff, and they all loved to hear her tell stories about her days as a nursing assistant in the hospital.

One day, she sat talking with one of them, and she was nearly in tears as she described each miscarriage she had, one by one. The woman had asked her if the daughter that came to visit was her only child. While the activities of the present day and the day before were often muddled in her brain, those early years and the details of them were like vivid colors painted onto a canvas, clear and as dark or beautiful as they had been on the day of creation.

The first miscarriage was the least dramatic, occurring at the beginning of the second trimester. She had simply begun to bleed, and the bleeding had started out heavy and lightened as it came to an end like a regular menstrual cycle. Several of the miscarriages required dilation and curettage, and she explained the ordeals. During one procedure, she had felt every scrape, and it left her with an infection that made her wish to die.

As she was telling the stories, Eve walked in for a visit and sat listening to the sultry voice of her mother. The expression on Gia's face and silver locks hanging down past her shoulders gave her a regal look, and the lighting was perfect against her milk-chocolate skin. Eve took out her camera as she listened to the stories, snapping shots of her mother and the staff members who stood listening to her. Some of them shed tears and others held pity in their eyes. Gia talked about the heartache that comes with the realization that as a woman, you cannot do the one thing you were on this earth to do.

"What was wrong with me? Had I done something to offend God?"

She lost hope with each passage of blood and

clots. While making it into the second trimester was usually a time to breathe a sigh of relief, all of her losses had occurred in that period, so she never believed she would become a mother. Not even with that last pregnancy, she explained to them. Throughout the last one, she had waited month by month, week by week, for the bloody termination when life left her body once again. She had not purchased baby clothes or a bassinet, and did not think of baby names as she had done in the past. She waited patiently for what she knew would come. She did not place her hand on her stomach to feel the movements that she felt so strong and alive by the sixth month.

Luther, who had been as discouraged as she was, told her, "Baby, it's OK. You're so far along now. We're gonna have a baby this time."

Gia knew better. It was not in the cards for her to carry a child to delivery. At six-and-a-half months, she began to have cramping and pain in her lower back. She called to speak with her obstetrician, and the doctor advised her to drink plenty of fluids and get some rest. She did as she was told. She slept restlessly that night, tossing and turning with discomfort.

At two in the morning, she felt an overwhelming desire to have a bowel movement. When she pushed and felt the pain and pressure on her vagina, she screamed for Luther. He came running to her, and then ran back to the phone to dial 911. The baby was tiny and his skin translucent. Gia held him up in her hands as she sat on the toilet. Luther cut the umbilical cord, and they tied it off with a shoelace and wrapped him in a towel. Even as she held him there in her hands, watching the tiny chest rise and fall, she knew that life was leaving his body. She watched as the last breath occurred, and the tiny chest stopped moving. She sat there on the toilet and passed the placenta that held the tiny baby.

"Baby number eight, the closest I ever came to having a child."

When the paramedics arrived, it was too late to even try to save the baby, and Gia had decided that this would be the last time.

"I couldn't put myself through that experience

again," she said. She decided to tie off the tubes that had carried seedlings to her fruitless womb and their untimely demise.

"Mom, that's not right. You had one more baby. Remember? Me!" Eve smiled, realizing that her mother was fading into one of her clouds.

Gia looked at her daughter; the big brown eyes transported her back to a different time and place. She remembered standing at the door of a clinic room and staring at her niece who lay on the table in a hospital gown. She walked in and closed the door behind her.

"Get up and get dressed. We're leaving."

"What?" Anita yelled. "I don't want to have this baby."

"I can't say I want you to have this baby either, but I don't want you to have to live with killing it. I know what it's like to have life growing inside of you, and then it's gone, and it's not a good feeling."

Anita sat up. She had made peace with the idea of getting rid of the baby, and now her aunt was telling her that she would regret it.

"There are other options. You can give the baby up for adoption. Plenty of women want to have kids and can't."

Gia inadvertently rubbed her stomach as she made the argument. She was only six weeks pregnant, but she thought of the losses that came before and how each one had stuck with her especially as she came to the realization that she might never carry a baby to term. She helped Anita dress quickly to leave. They took the same path back to the bus stop and to the apartment. Gia never told Luther that Anita did not go through with the abortion, not even after Gia's miscarriage at six months.

Her niece wore oversized clothing, and her small frame never grew very large, so only when she was naked could you tell she had a baby growing inside of her. Luther found out somehow and was angry that Anita, now eight months pregnant, would deliver his child and Gia would not. The baby growing inside her was like a judgment. He was guilty of impregnating his wife's young niece and fathering a child by her.

He began drinking that particular day with that thought in mind.

When he went over to Juanita's to pick up the girl, he only wanted to talk with her. He wanted to tell her that he was sorry and that he should never have touched her. When they got to the apartment, she sat down on the sofa. When he sat down next to her, she stood up abruptly. He moved toward her.

"Anita," he said as she pulled away and backed up to the other side of the room. "Leave me alone. I don't want you to touch me. If you touch me, I'm telling this time. I swear I am."

Luther didn't know what came over him. It wasn't his intention to grab her the way he did, and he tore the oversized T-shirt exposing her round belly.

Staring down at it he said, "You don't want me to touch you. You're carrying my baby, but now you don't want me to touch you."

He reached down to place his hand on her belly, to feel the baby growing inside. Anita slapped his hand away. Perhaps it was the alcohol or maybe the heroin, paired with the thirteen-year-old's rejection that caused him to snap. He slapped her hard, shaking her in his hands as he screamed at her.

"I'll touch you if I want to. Do you think your aunt can control me? Huh? Do you?"

He slapped her several times, ripping the sweat pants and underwear off as she tried to crawl away from him. Before he could stop himself, he had thrown her down onto the sofa, and she lay hunched over the ball that grew out in front of her. He pulled his penis from his pants and rammed it inside of her causing her to cry out in pain.

She begged, "Please don't, Uncle Luther, please. You'll hurt the baby. Please stop!"

Her cries angered him more, and he pummeled her small frame until she went limp. She lay there with her eyes closed not speaking or crying, and her breathing was shallow. Luther looked down to see what he had down to the girl, and he was horrified at what he saw.

"I'm so sorry. I'm so sorry," he said as he

backed out of the room toward the door. Anita didn't move. She lay still on the sofa even after he had closed the door behind him and left.

When Gia found her niece in the same spot, she didn't have to ask her what happened. Anita told her about Luther's attack, and Gia could not even shed a tear for her niece. She took her Anita to the bathroom and washed her body from head to toe, including the long black hair that she braided into ponytails on each side of her head. Gia dressed Anita in pajamas and took her back to bed. A few hours later, the girl awakened to a pool of blood and fluid all over her. She screamed for her aunt who came running from the back bedroom. They rushed to the hospital with Juanita driving the car. Tight cramps came in rapid succession, and Anita cried in pain.

"Hold on, baby. I'm gonna get you there!"

In the dayroom of the long term care facility, the staff dispersed as the storyteller grew silent. She looked out into the dayroom and a pleasant but absent expression came over her face. Her hands combed through the dreads, and she began to hum a song and then sing the words, "Raindrops on roses and whiskers on kittens." She hummed, sang, and smiled.

This was the way that it went. One moment Gia would be there, and the next she was gone. Her family was thankful to have glimpses of her, here and there, to be able to talk with her about things she remembered and listen to stories she never told before.

Eve called out to her mother again, "Mom?"

Gia looked up at the pretty, young woman in front of her and asked, "Hello, baby girl! Have we met?"

## CHAPTER TEN

Anita watched as her aunt seemed to die inside . The pregnant teenager had thought long and hard about adoption, and had remained uncomfortable with the idea of giving the baby away. How could she keep an eye on her child and make sure she was OK. Anita, realizing that she was also in no position to raise a baby of her own, decided that Gia should raise the little girl growing inside of her as her own.

What? I don't know if that's a good idea, Anita. What if people find out? How will we explain?"

Anita had been unrelenting,

"This is the best thing for everyone. You get to have a baby, and my baby doesn't have to grow up with some strangers. I'll never tell anyone. Do you think I want anyone to know her father is a…a….?"

"What about Luther?" Gia asked.

Anita frowned at her aunt. It amazed her how

much she had organized her life around Uncle Luther, while he held no regard for her when it came to his decisions.

"What about Luther? He is the father. He'll have to be a father."

The words burned her tongue as they exited her mouth, and she thought she would stay around to keep an eye on him. She could also see the pain that reality inflicted on Gia's face. Fate had decided to give Anita and Luther a baby, and she had decided to give the infant to Gia. She only needed her aunt to agree that this was the only option and the best thing for her child.

Luther was standing at the bathroom door when she came out that morning, preparing to go to Miss Juanita's house. She had already heard him leave and didn't expect him to be standing there. He startled her, and she jumped back losing a side of the towel she was holding in front of her, exposing her rounded stomach. She grabbed it quickly and ran across the hallway to the bedroom where she laid her clothes out on the bed. She dressed quickly and ran out of the apartment to Juanita's for the day.

Juanita knew about the pregnancy, but not that Luther was the father, so Anita kept it to herself until he saw her that morning. Even when Luther showed up at the door, announcing that he had come to pick her up, she didn't mention anything. She thought that he would question her about the pregnancy ask why she hadn't gotten the abortion, but she wanted to wait for Gia to tell him everything.

She smelled the alcohol on him and fear gripped her heart as he closed the apartment door behind them. She saw the moment his eyes turned wild and prayed that her aunt would come through the door before he could hurt her again. Gia arrived too late, and this time had been the worst of any. It had been full of anger and resentment. She wasn't surprised when she felt the warm gush between her legs, and the pain that started in her abdomen as it balled up into tight knots. She thought the baby was injured and dying from the attack. As Juanita drove the car with them to the hospital, Gia sat next to Anita in the backseat rubbing the girl's hair and kissing her face.

Anita thought that she was dying as she screamed, "Oh, my God! Get it out. I have to push it out!"

"Wait sweetheart not yet. Wait until we get to the hospital," Gia said.

Juanita sped to a screeching halt in the circle at the entrance of the maternity ward. Gia ran in to alert the front desk staff that her niece was in labor outside, and nurses rushed to the car with a wheelchair. They transferred Anita into the chair. Her bottom and legs were soaked, and a small spot with light-brown fluid was on her bottom as she stood and sat down again.

They rushed her inside where a triage nurse would evaluate her. When she removed the pajama pants and spread the girl's legs, the baby's head was peeking out. They took her upstairs in an elevator with no time for anesthesia.

"I'm right here, baby girl. Auntie is right here, OK."

Anita writhed in pain and wailed a pitiful,

"OK."

When they settled into the delivery room, the doctor stood directly in front of Anita, while Gia and Juanita held her legs back to ease the effort of pushing. The nurse explained to Anita that whenever she felt the contraction, or pain in her abdomen, she should push.

When the contractions began, they all counted, "One…two…three…" up to ten.

Each time they told Anita that the baby was right there, and they could see her.

"I can see the hair," Gia exclaimed excitedly.

After several minutes more and intense pressure, Anita pushed the baby out and she could hear the first cries. The umbilical cord dangled between them, and Gia took a pair of scissors to cut it. The baby appeared bluish-black at first but turned pinkish by the time a nurse took the newborn over to the warmer. A small bassinet with a light shining directly onto the infant was off to the side of the room. Several people Anita didn't recognize gathered with the nurse who had been attending to her. They began cleaning and suctioning the baby and the mother could see nurses administering a shot. When they were done, they brought the baby wrapped in a hospital blanket to Anita.

"It's a girl," the nurse said.

Anita looked down at her baby. She was all covered in something white and waxy, but she could see hair coating the baby's upper body, including a thick covering on her head that appeared straight now, but would later form tight black curls. She held her daughter close to her chest, and the baby girl opened her big, brown eyes... The baby had eyes like her mother's and like the aunt who would raise her. No one would question whether this was Gia's child.

Anita prayed to God that they had made the right decision. Gia signed formal adoption papers drawn up . Shortly after the birth and once more before Anita left the hospital, social workers came to ask her about the father of the baby. They asked repeatedly if it was someone she knew, and if they could do anything to help her?

Anita replied, "There was more than one boy,

and I'm not sure who the father is."

She hated lying, but she knew they would take the child away if she told the truth. Luther never came to the hospital. Perhaps, he was afraid that someone would find out and have him arrested for having a baby with a thirteen-year-old girl. The mother and baby stayed in the hospital for three days, the standard time for a first-time mother. Nurses came to Anita's room during the day and showed them how to bathe and feed the baby. Gia was there to help, but she allowed Anita to care for the baby, as well.

Juanita told her, "It's a wonderful thing you're doing for your aunt. Nobody deserves to be a mother more than her. Your baby is gonna have the best mother."

Anita knew Juanita meant well, but it saddened her to know that she could not be a mother to her baby. It saddened her more to know that Luther would be a father. He certainly hadn't earned the right to be a part of the child's life, and she wasn't sure he had any interest in doing so. He didn't see the baby until they got home. By then, Anita had begun to step back and allowed Gia to perform the tasks of a mother. Gia stayed at home for two months on family medical leave  after her legal adoption of the baby.

One evening, when they were alone together Gia had told Luther that they would be raising the baby after the child was born. She gave him no choice. He had impregnated her niece, and if he gave them any trouble, she would let the authorities know about it. Anita had asked her to raise the baby, to give her a good home, and that's what she intended to do. He needed very little reminding. The moment he set eyes on the baby, he was in love with her.

"She looks like me," he said. Anita and Gia both exchanged glances, but neither spoke. They went on like that living at home together, keeping their secret for days, then weeks, then years.

## CHAPTER ELEVEN

The guests filed into the church and moved along the pews as instructed, according to whether they were there for the bride or the groom. Several of Eve's church sisters were acting as ushers, escorting people through the aisles to their seats. Both sides were completely full as the music began to play.

Several people stood at the back of the church, not wanting to disrupt others to find an available space. One of them was a frail woman with a short, gray bob that hugged her face just below the chin. She looked around nervously, as though she thought she might fall over at any time. A gentleman sitting on the bride's side rose from his seat and called over for her to take his place.

At first, she shook her head and declined, "I'm fine, honey."

She then did as he insisted. Just as she sat down, the front doors opened and the procession began. Stevie Wonder's song "Ribbon in the Sky" filled the sanctuary as the ladies and their escorts walked up to the altar. Gia led the way and the tears that had begun to fill in her eyes before the doors opened and only temporarily halted started again. As she walked down the aisle, she looked ahead at the man who would become her son-in-law, and she couldn't be happier that she was entrusting her baby girl to him. Gia grinned and scanned the crowd of faces, so happy that so many people were there to celebrate with them.

As she looked to her left, she caught a glimpse of a face that almost took her breath away. Her feet stopped moving, until the young man by her side tugged gently at her arm. Each woman's eyes remained locked in a stare until Gia was too far ahead. The woman seated began to cry also, as she watched the back of the gold dress move down the aisle, the scarf waving good-bye to her. When the song ended and a different tune began to play, she turned her attention once again to the door. She inhaled deeply as the bride crossed the threshold. The young woman was breathtaking.

Her bright eyes and brown skin were perfect, and the dress she wore appeared as though an artist had sculpted it onto her. More tears came now as the woman watched the bride march down the aisle and meet up with Gia.

"Who gives this woman away?" the short, handsome pastor asked.

"I do," Gia said with conviction, and she pecked her daughter on the cheek as she passed to go take the seat reserved just for her. Gia glanced at the back of the sanctuary, but the surprise guest was gone. Perhaps, it had only been her imagination, or, more likely, her slippery mind playing tricks on her. Hallucinations were a new symptom that she could add to her list. Yet she couldn't help but wonder if she had imagined what she had seen. It wasn't as though she was sure she saw the person she knew so many years ago. The woman had aged quite a bit and didn't look as Gia would have imagined after so many years.

"It is the job of all of you who are present to bear witness to this union, to remind these two of the promise they made to each other. Tell them in those difficult times ahead to think back to this day, when they swore before all of you, and God, to remain committed to each other."

Gia's mind returned to the present, and she listened as the pastor spoke of not mixing "new wine" with the "old wine." He talked of starting fresh, from that moment on and loving each other through any trials. She thought of her own marriage and all of the baggage that had come along with her and Luther. They had taken a tub and filled it with so much old wine, she couldn't tell if any part of it were new. Her thoughts took her through all of their years together, and the last picture that flashed before her was Luther laying there dying, reaching out for her.

"God forgive me," she whispered.

She looked at Eve standing there today beaming at the front of the altar, and she prayed that this new wine would come out much better than the old wine that came before it -- that it would not be bitter and spoiled.

"Miss Gia?"

The young escort was beckoning her to take his arm once again. The ceremony had ended, and the wedding party hurried up the aisle toward the door and the Rolls Royce waiting outside. The woman Gia thought she saw was not sitting there at the back of the church. She had disappeared as abruptly as she had appeared.

The newlyweds and wedding party took many pictures before entering the country club ballroom for the reception. The bride even had her own camera on hand and occasionally grabbed it to take snapshots of her own. It was a habit. The place was exquisite. Each table had a small square vase holding lilies in assorted colors, and each flower had a shimmering jewel in the center. Large floodlights shot rays of orange, red, and yellow across the room, creating an arch that covered the entire hall. Guests dined on pan-seared salmon and baked chicken with asparagus and garlic potatoes. A chocolate fondue fountain with assorted fruits and cakes for dipping stood on a table to the side. Family and friends ate until their stomachs were full, and then they danced.

The first dance was for the bride and, in this case, her mother. Gia and Eve danced to the song "Mama" by Boys II Men, and they laughed and looked into each other's eyes like a couple of silly schoolgirls .

When the song was over, the deejay announced that the bride and groom would now share their first dance as husband and wife. As Nathan walked toward her, Eve realized that her mother stopped short of exiting the dance area. She was staring ahead into the crowd of onlookers.

Eve turned to Nathan and whispered, "Just a minute, babe."

Making her way over to her mother, she said, "Momma, you OK?" Her daughter's voice startled Gia. "Uh, yes, yes, I'm fine. I just thought…."

She peered off in the direction she had been staring, searching the crowd.

"Momma," the daughter whispered again.

Sensing the concern in her daughter's voice, Gia focused on her gaze, "I'm sorry. It's getting late and I should probably get going. I couldn't be more proud of you, and I want you to have a wonderful honeymoon, and tell me all about it when you get back ."

"I will, Momma. I promise, and if you need anything, you make sure you call me because I'll have my phone the whole time."

"I will do no such thing. You leave that phone and enjoy every moment. You can't get these moments back sweetheart."

The two embraced each other tightly and Eve buried her face in her mother's neck.

"I love you, Momma! Thank you so much for being with me today."

Gia just nodded, knowing exactly what her daughter meant. Eve signaled to the young man who had been Gia's escort during the ceremony. He was Nathan's friend and an employee, a young man her husband had taken on and begun mentoring when he saw the potential he possessed.

"Jared, will you please take my mother back home now?"

They had arranged earlier for him to do so.

Before they left, she saw her mother looking back from the ballroom door at her and Nathan, as they danced to the Coltrane song her father loved so much. "My Favorite Things."


Eve was so happy with the way the day had turned out. Her mother had stood there in front of the church and gave her away, teary-eyed and joyful. Nathan, her love, had told her that everything would be all right.

"Have faith, baby. It's brought us this far." The ceremony was amazing, and they couldn't have chosen a better location than the country club to have the reception. The flowers and decorations were splendid, and the guests feasted on a wonderful meal.

Uncle Mitch had been too weak to attend the wedding, but if he had been there, he would have also given her away. She would call and speak with him before she left for the Cayman Islands the next afternoon.

Gia walked into her bedroom at the Manor,

happy and exhausted from the wedding festivities. On the bed by the window, Mitch lay fast asleep. She was glad that he was able to rest, because lately he had been in so much pain that he found it hard to fall asleep or sleep long when he did. She turned toward her own bed and reached to set the scarf down, and there was the woman whom she had seen earlier.

"Hello, big sister," Jess said aloud. Mitch shuffled some on the bed, and Gia realized she was not hallucinating.

"It's really you!"

Gia walked toward the woman and ran a hand along her face, cupping the chin between her thumb and forefinger. The puddles formed in Gia's eyes and overflowed onto her face as she cried for what seemed to be the hundredth time that day.

"I've missed you so very much ," she said to Jessica.

The two sisters embraced and both shook with joy as they hugged hard enough to make up for forty-six years of lost time.

"How did you find me?" Gia said. "Where have you been all this time? Oh, dear God, I have so much to tell you."

Jessica laughed as she said, "I haven't been far. Believe it or not, I've lived in Philadelphia most of this time. I suppose I thought of Anita and you, and figured I have more time behind me than I do ahead of me. So many times over the years I thought of looking for you, but I always found some excuse to stay away."

Gia instantly became somber, "I've got something to tell you."

The sister spoke through pursed lips, "I already know. I had a friend help me search for you all on the Internet, and I found an obituary for Anita in the News Journal archives. Why would I expect that after all I'd done that, I wouldn't have some price to pay? I just didn't know how high a price until I saw that obituary."

Gia's look did not change. She didn't expect her sister to know that her child had died long ago, but she knew she had much more to tell her.

"There's more!"

She asked Jessica to walk with her to the common area, and they sat for hours as she poured her heart out for the first time to anyone other than Emma about everything that had happened throughout the years. Jessica cried and her small frame seemed to shrink with every crushing detail of her daughter's life and subsequent death.

"Luther, he…I caught him with Anita, when she was twelve."

Gia paused watching the expression on her sister's face, but Jessica didn't so much as blink, and she kept quiet.

"They were on the bed, and he was having sex with her. I…I…I was so shocked Jess. I never thought he would do anything to her, but I didn't see it or realize what was happening."

Tears flooded in Gia's eyes and all of the guilt she felt the day her niece died came rushing back to her. She never expected to have to explain it to Anita's mother, and for the first time, she had to own the responsibility for the way things had turned out.

"I didn't protect her, and then we found out she was pregnant."

Jess still had not moved, but she too was crying silently. She sat stoic, waiting for Gia to continue the story.

"I know this is a lot to take in all at one time, and I wouldn't tell you any of it, if I didn't think you needed to know."

Gia wiped her face with a handkerchief she had tucked in her brassiere. "We were both pregnant at the same time. My son -- the child I was carrying -- never made it."

Gia began to sob, and she collected herself, preparing to tell her sister the most vital information.

"But Anita had a baby. My daughter, Eve is actually your granddaughter, Jess. She's Anita's baby girl. Nita asked me to raise her. She thought I could do a better job than she could, being so young. Lord knows why she believed that."

The tears had stopped falling, and Gia's words moved forward in time.

"Then, eleven years later, I walked in on that

bastard standing over Eve, ready to pounce on her while she lay there asleep and helpless."

She grew angrier now, remembering the stench of alcohol and Luther standing over the child.

"His own goddamn daughter! I ran at him that time. I tried to keep him off her. Then the motherfucker turned on me, and he probably would have killed me, too, except he slipped and hit his head on the counter."

She took a deep breath and looked directly into her sister's eyes.

"Nita came in just as I was checking on Eve, who was still fast asleep. Then Luther started to shake and went into a seizure. Well, baby sister, then I did one of the worse things I've done in my whole life. I watched him die, and didn't let Nita call 911 like she wanted to."

She shook her head as the wrinkled brow on her sister's face formed the question.

"Yes, I killed a man, and I thought that only I would have to pay for that sin, but I was wrong."

Her hands began to shake now and the sobbing began again.

"Anita was so angry with me for not protecting her, and she stayed around, to be close to her daughter. I think it just ate her up inside that, even though I let her get hurt, I was all she had. One day, she started to whip my ass so bad, and I just let her. I thought maybe if she could get it out of her, maybe she could move forward. I would have let her pound on me forever if it did her any good."

Jess moved for the first time, placing her hand on her sister's.

"Tell me what happened," she said softly.

She lifted Gia's chin so that they were eye to eye once again.

"I closed my eyes, she was about to hit me again, and I heard something, felt her tense up then let go. She fell down on me and I saw...Eve...."

Gia handed a piece of paper to her sister, and Jess began to read it carefully. She sat holding the letter Gia had written for Eve, the one she had drafted in a moment of fear. It occurred to her that she might forget everything before she got a chance to tell Eve the truth, or worse, she might tell her without realizing who she was. She had held many conversations that she couldn't remember with people she barely knew. The letter had spared all of the worse details, but said that Anita was her biological mother and that she had been raped and gotten pregnant. She wanted to explain to her why Anita had been so angry without burdening Eve with the sins of her father.

"I just couldn't bring myself to tell her that she killed her own mother. She already has such a hard time believing she killed her cousin. She loved Nita. She was just a little girl, and she was afraid. We kept so many secrets that they tore us apart."

Before she sealed the gold envelope, she had changed her mind and written a different letter that she placed inside with a check.

One of the nursing assistants passed by, "Is everything OK?"

She was asking Jess, realizing that both women were crying and that one was suffering from Alzheimer's.

"No, but then everything is never OK, young lady," Jess said.

The nurse looked puzzled, but she continued on, satisfied that she could do nothing to help them. Jess sat staring off into space for what seemed an eternity.

When she looked back at Gia, she said, "No, she's your daughter, and she is my niece. I may not have been able to give my daughter a mother who loved her, but I will not take that away from my granddaughter. She may well just be the one thing that has come out right out of everything I've ever done. Maybe there has been mercy after all."

Jessica told Gia all about what happened after she left the hospital. How she had stopped in the bathroom on the way outside to smoke, and that looking at herself in the mirror, she knew she was no good to any one, especially that sick baby in the NICU nursery. Jess had gone outside and started walking away from the hospital. Out on the roadway, she had been picked up by a man and went home with him. She never looked back, until now. Her life had been filled with drugs, crazy people, and one bad choice after another.

She confessed, "That girl would have probably had a much worse life, and probably wouldn't have lived as long as she did if she had been with me. Every year she spent on this earth was a gift."

Gia held her sister's hand. "I'm so sorry."

Jess shook her head, "Me too, me too."

Gia hugged her again. "How long are you staying?"

"I'm going back tonight, but I'll be back. I've been thinking of moving back this way."

At that moment, a part of Gia that had been broken long ago mended itself.

"We can take a different road into tomorrow."

Jess nodded in agreement. The two sat up the whole night talking, and when Jess left the next morning, Gia could still remember all that had transpired the night before. She thanked God for keeping her lucid when she needed it most.

Eve and Nathan climbed out of the Rolls Royce and he lifted her up in his arms, "What kind of man would I be if I didn't carry my bride across the threshold for the first time?"

She smiled, and he kissed her on the lips. His strong arms held her firmly, and she knew he would never let her fall. He climbed the stairs, instead of taking the elevator, to the apartment, still carrying her, kissing her and nudging his face against hers the entire way.

"I'm so glad we found each other. I can't imagine my life without you."

Eve pressed her face against his, her arms wrapped around his neck as they entered the apartment. "You wouldn't have to. We were meant to be in each other's lives. That's why we are."

"Welcome home, Mrs. Nathan Townsend."

He kissed her once again as he lowered her to the floor, and she kicked off her shoes, standing on her tiptoes to continue their sensual exchange. They kissed each other passionately, holding on tight until finally they had to release each other.

"I'm gonna get out of my dress," she breathed heavily, her eyes narrowed to brown slits like a feline. She purred as she walked in the direction of the bedroom. Nathan kept his eyes on her as he switched on the lights and then dimmed them. He watched her, and she glanced over her shoulder as she bent forward removing the dress. Underneath, she was wearing a cream-colored bustier and matching underwear with blue silk trim.

"You are so sexy!" Nathan exclaimed.

He walked up behind her pressing his solid erection against the silk panties. He pushed his right hand down into the camisole grabbing at the ample breast and pulling it free from its bondage.

"I'll never understand how I ended up with someone as wonderful as you are."

From over her shoulder, he reached his mouth toward the nipple. The warm tingling sensation made her vaginal muscles contract, and she pushed back against the heat in his pants.

"Finders keepers," she whispered softly.

Nathan played with the small mound pulsating between her thighs with his left hand, making circular motions as he applied gentle pressure.

She grabbed his hand pushing it harder against

her flesh, and said, "Put your fingers inside."

He obliged and bit softly into the curve where her neck and shoulders met. She moaned pushing harder against the hand between her legs. He released the breast and pushed down on her back as her hair fell toward the ground. He ran his fingers along the lace trim of her panties than snatched them down below her bottom. Then he continued to massage the lips of her vagina with his left hand. He pushed his right hand between her thighs from behind and used it to spread her legs. He played with her from behind, inserting one, then two fingers, testing to see how well-lubricated she had become. When he was satisfied that she was ready, he released his erection from his pants and guided his thick penis inside of her.

"Oh! Yes!" Nathan exclaimed as he slowly grinded into her, massaging her clit and holding firmly on to her shoulder.

Eve began to shudder, and she reached her arms forward holding the floor for support. An electric current began at her clitoris and grew more intense as it spread through the rest of her body. She pushed her hands against the ground, moving her forward, and then dropping herself back hard, she squeezed her vaginal muscles tight around him.

"Yes, yes, yes!"

A smile crossed her lips as she heard his reaction to her performance. His pleasure made the electricity more intense, and she reciprocated by slamming down harder each time she pushed her body forward and he thrust forward in unison.

"Oh, I love you so fucking much. Thank you for being my wife. Thank you! Thank you!"

He grabbed at her hair and held it firmly, and when he could no longer focus, his hand came from her clit and grabbed her around her waist squeezing so hard his nails dug into her flesh.

"Oh my God," she cried out from the pleasure of the pain.

Her cries grew louder and louder, and her body vibrated more vigorously. Nathan tossed his head back now, and he was pushing inside of her deeper than he ever had before. He reached down and grabbed both of her arms crossing them behind her back and pulling her straight up at the same time. He could feel her tighten in reaction to this change in position, and he pushed even harder as she stood nearly straight up in front of him, unable to move from his embrace, and she came vibrating like the number twelve train.

"Ahhhhhh," he roared as his dick pulsed, and he ejaculated inside of her.

He pulled her waist toward him and quivered with each pulse. Finally, he was still. Sweat was dripping off him onto her back and she relaxed against his chest. They stood there spent, and he kissed her on the back of her head and neck with arms wrapped around her waist.

"I love you, I love you, I love you," he said to his wife.

He massaged her arms and thighs, and she could feel the heat rising between them again. They were facing the low, white table now, and for the first time Eve noticed something new in their apartment. Sitting on top of the table, against the vase, was a gold envelope. The words written on it were in cursive and read: "To My Baby Girl ." She planned to open it when they finished. However, she forgot and the letter sat unopened when they left the next morning for their honeymoon.

Eve began to worry immediately when she got home from their honeymoon and saw that her mother had called the house four times already that day. It wasn't like Gia to call at all let alone repeatedly. She hadn't expected her mother to sound so happy on the phone, and she certainly hadn't expected the news Gia wanted to share with her.

"My sister found me. Your Aunt Jessica is alive."

It took a minute for the words to register, and even after they did, she wondered if her mother was having one of her moments.

"What?" she asked her mother.

"My sister is alive, I thought I saw her at your wedding, but I wasn't sure. Then she was here in my room when I got back. She's alive, and she wants to meet you."

Eve grew silent at the other end of the phone. It had been many years since she thought of her Aunt Jess, whom she had never met. In her mind, the woman had been dead long ago, and now with her resurrection, came the emergence of feelings she had put behind her long ago. She saw herself, eleven years old standing there holding the knife in her hand.

She could see her mother holding her cousin, Anita, and the words rang in her ears, "What have you done?"

"Hello," Gia said at the other end of the line.

"Does she know?"

Gia could hear the desperation in Eve's voice, and she felt bad realizing that this would not be as easy for her daughter as it had been for her.

"Baby that was a long time…"

Eve interrupted her "Momma! Does she know what happened?"

Gia was taken aback by her daughter's outburst. Even as an adult, Eve had always been very respectful, never raising her voice in anger.

"Does Aunt Jess know that I killed her

daughter?"

Nathan was opening the luggage to take out the dirty clothes, and he put the other things away. When Eve began to shout, he walked up behind her and started to rub her shoulders. She pulled away from him, holding the phone against her ear with both hands.

"She knows everything, Eve. Sweetheart, she knows more than you do, but she has come to peace with all of the bad in life, and we are what family she has left. She wants to meet you," Gia said.

The line was silent and tears formed in Eve's eyes. "How can I...I don't know if I can look her in her eyes."

"You can, baby. We all make mistakes, and she is not judging you."

Gia paused to allow time for her words to sink in. "She is your family, and she needs to meet you just as much as you need to meet her. It's running away from our problems that takes us to places we should never be. Trust me. I know a lot about that! I'm not gonna preach to you, but she'll be by tomorrow afternoon, and we'll wait for you to come until dinnertime. After that she's going back to her home, and I don't know how she'll take it if you don't show up here."

Eve heard the phone click on the other end. She could tell her mother was angry, but she thought about her Aunt Jessica. How could she not hate her, or at least be angry with her? Jess had finally come back after all these years to find out someone had killed her child. Did it matter who that someone was? Can anybody love a person who killed his or her own child?

"Baby," Nathan called her softly, but still startled her out of her thoughts, "I have to agree with your mother on this."

He had heard Gia through the phone because her voice was loud, and her anger amplified the sound. Eve walked into the kitchen and opened the refrigerator door, taking out a carton of orange juice and checking the date on it before pouring some into a tall glass.

"I mean, your aunt has been gone for years, and don't forget, she left her daughter when she was only a baby. I imagine she's had to do a whole lot of soul searching to face your mother or any of you. I can't imagine that someone taking steps to mend broken fences after decades would come bearing an axe."

He walked around to where she was standing and stared at her, crossing his arms in front of his chest.

The next day, Eve sank down into the leather interior of the BMW while Nathan drove them to the home where her aunt and mother were waiting for her arrival. She could smell the leather hide as if he had just driven the car off the lot. It was actually six years old, but Nathan cared for it as if it was a baby. If it snowed outside, he would leave it parked and they would both drive in Eve's Honda to keep his car from getting weather damage. The leather smell and the way the seats absorbed heat were comforting. It was like sitting on her mother's lap on a summer day.

Eve looked out at the trees that lined the park and the sign that announced the ice cream festival would start soon. She remembered going to the festival as a child, watching the fireworks and eating mint-chocolate-chip ice cream sundaes. All of those memories, the happy childhood ones, had both her father and Anita somewhere in the background.

Nita used to go with them almost everywhere, even though she would sulk and complain the entire time. She tried not to think about her much, but she still couldn't understand her cousin. She could have made a choice to be happy, but she chose to be angry with everyone all of the time. More than anything, Eve wished she knew the truth about what happened the night her father died. She was sure that she didn't know the real story, only the one that had been concocted and fed to the police, the neighbors, and her for the rest of her life.

She had loved her father with all of the unconditional and protective love that a daughter could muster. It wasn't until the day she almost fell victim to men under the influence of the same alcohol and drugs that her father partook of that she realized how he might have appeared to everyone else. She still loved him dearly, but perhaps her father was not the valiant knight she had imagined he was.

She thought more and more about those nights when she would dream he was there standing over her. In the day, she was never afraid of him, but in those dreams, he didn't look at her like a loving father. She was as afraid in those dreams as she was with her face pressed against that putrid mattress in the crack house. Perhaps Anita was no saint, but then neither was her father. Eve considered the idea that something else was the reason for Anita's tears that night, and her mother's insistence that she leave their home.

Nathan pulled the car into the circular driveway and stopped directly in front of the entrance. Over to the side was a small concrete deck with patio tables and chairs under umbrellas for the residents to spend time outside getting fresh air. Eve could see her mother sitting next to a woman who looked a lot like her. She could see the face of her older cousin in that woman's face, as well. Eve looked over at Nathan who had not turned off the car or put it in park.

"Aren't you coming?"

He shook his head, "In a minute, I'm going to park the car in the lot. Go ahead, babe, you'll be fine."

Eve looked down at her lap, at the gold envelope with the letter her mother had written. She had forgotten about it until they returned from the honeymoon. It was still sitting on the table near their bed. It almost sounded like her mother was saying goodbye:

*To My Baby Girl,*

*Every day that goes by, I lose a little more of myself. The only thing that keeps me from losing my mind completely is the thought of you and of how wonderful you turned out. I was supposed to be the one to guide you in life and show you unconditional love, but you were the one who taught me. When I thought that I had taken all that I could bear and was ready to throw in the towel, you pulled me back into the fight. I can only thank God that I was chosen to be your mother. I didn't deserve you, and surely, I didn't make all of the right choices, but before I forget everything that ever meant anything to me, I want you to know I love you more than anything in this world. When God sent you, he sent me an angel. I would rather have spent one minute remembering you than to remember an entire lifetime without you in it. My love, if there is one thing I wish you would take from me, it's never to let the past ruin your future. Nothing good comes from regret. You have been seeing the world through the lens of your camera and capturing its beauty since you were five years old. Don't ever forget that also you have the ability to make life beautiful. It is the thing that I admire so much about you. You've been doing that since the day you were born. I love you always, even if I can't remember!*

*Sincerely Yours,*

*Momma*

Eve fought back tears and tried to steady her breathing and keep her heart from racing. She stepped out of the car, locking eyes with Nathan as she turned to close the door. He gave her a knowing grin, and it was as if she felt his hands reaching down to help her up as he had done years ago. She turned around and walked toward the two ladies sitting at the first table.

"Hello," she said as she approached.

Jess stood up, She took two steps forward, and then opened her arms wide to hug Eve, rocking her back and forth in her arms. Eve could feel her body shake, and she knew that the woman was crying. She lost the fight to ward off her own tears, and they streamed down her cheeks, soaking the shoulder of her aunt's blouse. After several minutes, they backed away but clasped hands.

"I'm so sorry." Eve said.

"Shhh! Hush, girl. We're gonna leave the past where it belongs."

Jess smiled, and Eve could see and hear her cousin in this familiar stranger. She looked down at her mother and said, "Hey, Momma!"

Gia had been watching the two the entire time without uttering a word. She wore a smile of contentment and a veil of peace. Her brow wrinkled in confusion.

"Hello, young lady. You look so much like your mother." She looked back and forth between Eve and Jessica. "You're very lucky. I always wanted to have a daughter."

# ABOUT THE AUTHOR

Lowan Anderson is a freelance writer and registered
nurse. She is a veteran of the U.S. Air Force and
currently works for a non-profit health clinic. Her first
published work was an article written for the Air Force
detailing the construction of a morale center for
troops in Iraq. Lowan is the mother of two boys and
resides in Wilmington, Delaware.